CAN THEY SURVIVE DEAD MAN'S DROP?

"Tori!" Nichelle shouted, but it was too late; Tori had missed the drop-off and was already lurching skyward toward a sign with a big black diamond on it.

"What are we going to do?" Ana said. The drop was quickly approaching.

"I don't know about you, Ana, but I'm getting off. I'm no advanced skier. Get ready!"

But Ana shook her head. "Nichelle, I can't let Tori go alone. I'm staying on."

Nichelle barely had time to give Ana a wide-eyed "good luck!" before she jumped from the chair and tucked into position for her intermediate run.

"Ana!" someone shouted. She was just able to catch a glimpse of Blaine's shocked face, staring in disbelief at her, before she lurched up and away again, following Tori up the mountain.

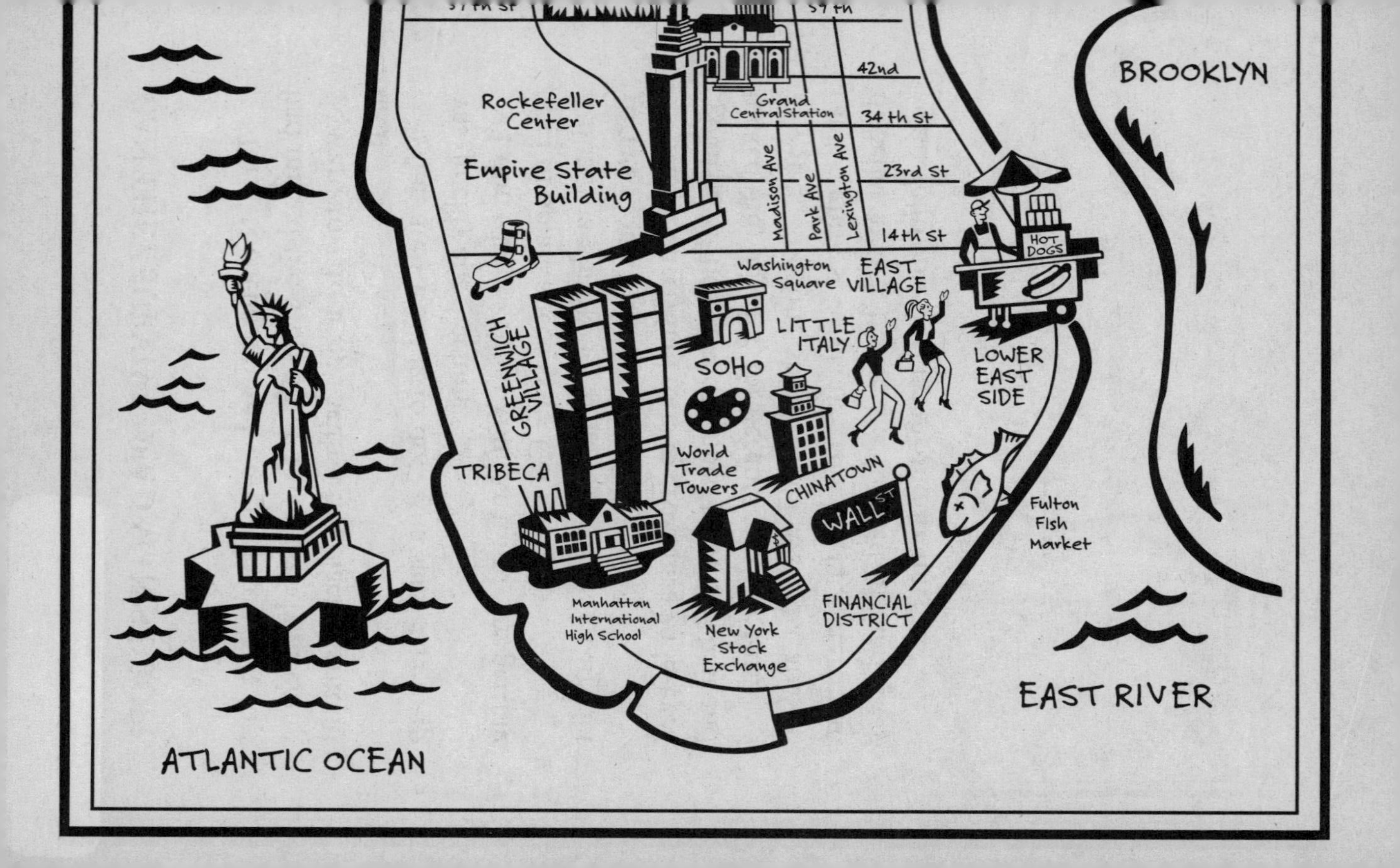
Rockefeller Center
Empire State Building
Grand Central Station
42nd
34 th St
23rd St
14th St
Madison Ave
Park Ave
Lexington Ave
BROOKLYN
HOT DOGS
Washington Square
EAST VILLAGE
GREENWICH VILLAGE
LITTLE ITALY
SOHO
LOWER EAST SIDE
TRIBECA
World Trade Towers
CHINATOWN
WALL ST
Fulton Fish Market
Manhattan International High School
New York Stock Exchange
FINANCIAL DISTRICT
EAST RIVER
ATLANTIC OCEAN

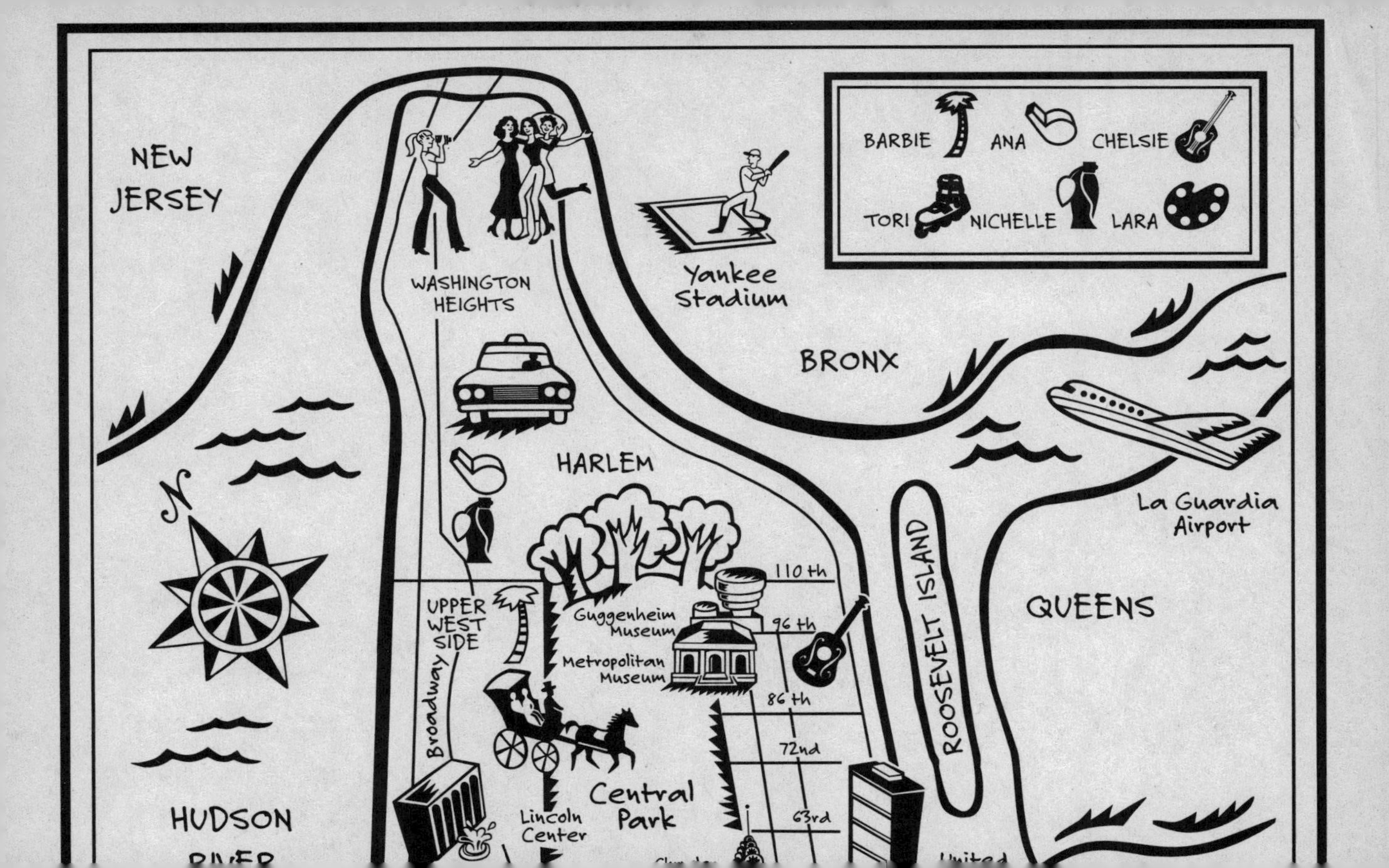
NEW JERSEY
BARBIE
ANA
CHELSIE
TORI
NICHELLE
LARA
WASHINGTON HEIGHTS
Yankee Stadium
BRONX
HARLEM
La Guardia Airport
110 th
96 th
86 th
72nd
63rd
UPPER WEST SIDE
Broadway
Guggenheim Museum
Metropolitan Museum
ROOSEVELT ISLAND
QUEENS
Central Park
Lincoln Center
HUDSON

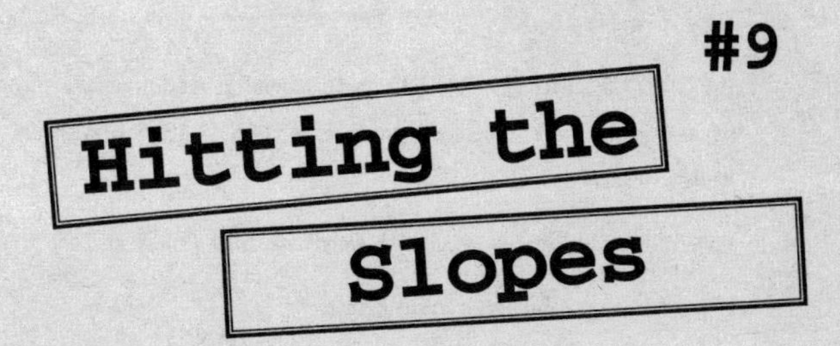

By Melanie Stewart

A GOLD KEY PAPERBACK
Golden Books Publishing Company, Inc.
New York

A GOLD KEY Paperback Original

Golden Books Publishing Company, Inc.
888 Seventh Avenue
New York, NY 10106

Cover photography by Graham Kuhn

Interior art by Amy Bryant

ISBN: 0-307-23458-4

First Gold Key paperback printing December 1999

10 9 8 7 6 5 4 3 2 1

Printed in the U.S.A.

GENERATI*N
GIRL

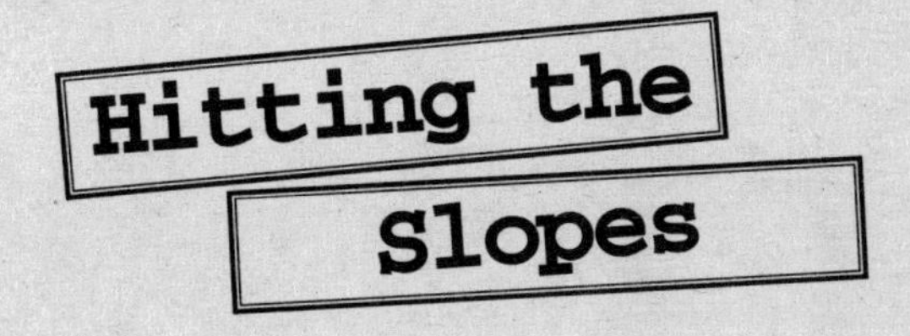
Hitting the
Slopes

Skiing, Anyone?

"I've got to find a new sport," Ana Suarez muttered to herself, licking a snowflake from her lip as she rounded the track into the last lap of her early morning workout. A serious athlete, Ana usually relished her early morning runs, delighting in the play of wind and sun upon her face, but today the snow had soaked her sneakers and turned her feet numb with cold.

As the finish line approached, Ana sprinted the last fifty yards, then made a beeline for the ground-level entrance to the athletic facilities at International High School. She swiped her student ID through the scanner and sighed with relief as the door swung open into the cozy warmth of the workout room. She took a fast shower, changed into her school clothes and shoes, then headed up to her locker on the second floor.

A number of teachers were already at work behind their desks. The only sound Ana heard as she walked to her locker was the sound of her shoes on the floor. Then a familiar voice called out behind her.

"Good mornink, Ms. Ana."

Ana turned to see Mr. Pugachev, the school janitor, leaning out of a doorway, mop and bucket in hand.

"Good morning, Poogy. Sorry to mess up your nice floor," Ana said apologetically. "It's snowing like crazy out there."

The janitor shrugged and smiled. "Not to sweat, my friend. I am making the mop-up." Poogy's English had definitely improved since Ana had first met him, but it still had a long way to go. "In Russia, where I am coming from, we are used to much snow," he continued. He stared at Ana's feet. "I think what you need is — how do you say it? —

shoe-snows." Poogy grinned, looking quite pleased with himself.

Ana hid a smile. "It's *snowshoes*, Poogy, and if this weather keeps up, we'll all need them to get around. Well, *Das-vidanya*," she said, which she knew meant "see you later" in Russian.

"Sure," Poogy said with a nod. "Take them easy."

Ana gazed at the clock on the wall in her first-period English class. It was 8:17 A.M. — three minutes before the late bell — and her Australian friend Tori Burns hadn't arrived yet. Tori sat next to Ana, and generally the two of them liked to get to class early so that they could spend time together. Their friendship was an unusual one, based on deep respect for each other's skills and abilities. Yet while they shared many natural talents, their personalities and interests were remarkably different. Ana was a disciplined athlete who excelled at competitive sports. She was considered the rising star on I. H.'s track team and was looking forward to joining the swim team in the spring. Tori, on the other hand, cared little for team sports, but she was still a superb athlete.

At the front of the room, Mr. Toussaint, Ana's English teacher, sorted some papers on his desk, waiting for the period to begin. He was a good-looking African-American with slightly graying hair and twinkly brown eyes. He was revered by many I. H. students as the best teacher in school.

With only seconds to spare, Tori sailed through the door, huffing and puffing, looking an absolute mess. Her ponytails had come undone and her long blond hair was flying every which way. Her clothes were wet and her jeans were torn at both knees. Her normally pretty face was beet-red and twisted into a grimace as she hobbled to her desk and sat stiffly down.

Ana stared at her in amazement. "Tori, are you okay?" she whispered.

"Crikey," Tori whispered back. "This white stuff sure is pretty," she said, nodding toward the window, where blankets of snow covered the ground. "It's not so good for bladin', though," and she showed Ana the scrapes on her knees and elbows.

Ana gasped. "Are you all right?" she whispered. "Maybe you should see the nurse."

Tori wrinkled her nose. "Just a few scratches is

all. We don't get much snow back home — I'm not used to it."

Ana smiled, "Nobody's used to in-line blading in the snow, Tori."

The bell rang and Mr. Toussaint stood up and began chalking something at the blackboard. When he finished, he cleared his throat loudly. "Good morning, class," he said in his booming baritone, then asked, "Would anyone care to read aloud the quote I've written on the board? What — no volunteers? How about you, Tori?"

Tori grinned, "No worries, Mr. Toussaint. 'At Christmas I no more desire a rose,'" she read, "'Than wish a snow in May's new-fangled mirth; But like of each thing that in season grows.' That's dingo, Mr. T. Who wrote that?"

Mr. Toussaint smiled. "I'm glad you like it," he said. "As to who wrote it, I was hoping one of you might tell *me*."

Ana raised her hand. "It sounds like Shakespeare," she said.

Mr. Toussaint nodded. "Very good, Ana. Now perhaps you'd be kind enough to tell us what the verse means?"

Ana read the words again, blinked a few times,

then smiled. "I think it means we shouldn't complain about the snow, any more than we'd complain about flowers in May. Is that right?"

Mr. Toussaint smiled and nodded deeply. "That's it exactly," he said. "Now open your books to page 328. . . ."

After class, Ana helped Tori out into the hall where they bumped into their friends Barbie Roberts and Chelsie Peterson.

Barbie's jaw dropped instantly. "My goodness, Tori," she said. "What happened?"

Tori shrugged. "Bit of a bingle," she said, using an Australian expression for accident. "No major damage."

Chelsie rolled her eyes. "Don't tell me you tried to skate here in the snow!"

"I'm afraid she did," Ana said, "not that I had much better luck on the track this morning — I nearly got frostbite!"

Chelsie shook her head. "You're both *mad*, if you ask me," she said in her proper British accent.

"Exactly how bad are your injuries, Tori?" Barbie asked.

"I'll mend," Tori said.

"Do you think you'll be okay by next weekend?"

"Crikey!" Tori said. "This girl's made of steel. All I need are two days."

"Hey, wait a minute," Ana interjected. "What's next weekend?"

"Our magical skiing weekend," Barbie replied with a grin.

Ana, Tori, and Chelsie threw her blank stares.

"Here, look!" Barbie said. She reached into her bookbag and took out a flyer. "This was posted by the sophomore ski club," she said. "It says they have ten spaces still open for their big ski trip to Vermont next weekend. And I was thinking that if all four of us signed up, and if we got Nichelle and Lara and Blaine and Randall and the Pants Boys to go, we could take those spaces and have a really great time."

"Dunno," Tori said. "I've never been."

"Me neither," Ana said.

"I don't believe it!" Chelsie exclaimed. "You two sports fanatics have never gone skiing, *ever*?"

Ana and Tori shook their heads.

"Oh, you must try it," Chelsie continued. "My parents used to take me to the Alps every winter — it was great fun. I know you two would love it."

The hallway traffic was thinning out as students filed into their second-period classrooms. "We'd better get going," Ana said, "or we'll be late."

Barbie raised her hand as if it were a stop sign. "Hold it," she said. "Nobody goes anywhere until everybody promises to go skiing together."

"I'll go," Chelsie said. "I haven't been skiing for ages!"

"Me too!" Tori exclaimed. "I'm game!"

"Ana?" Barbie asked.

Always the practical one in the group, Ana had absolutely no idea how she would find the time, not to mention the finances, for such a trip, especially with Christmas coming. Even so she felt herself being swept up in the tide of Barbie's enthusiasm.

"Okay — count me in," she said.

The four friends cheered.

Ana tugged on Tori's arm. "Come on," she said, "or we'll be late for math!"

"I'll ask Nichelle!" Barbie called after them. "And I'll leave Lara a note. Let's work out the details in the I. H. *Generation Beat* office after school!"

"It's a date!" Ana shouted, pulling the still-limping Tori down the hall and ducking into math class just as the bell rang.

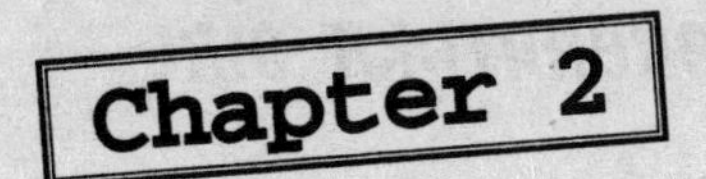

Chaperone Number Two

By seventh period Ana was feeling tired. It had been a long day. It didn't help matters that Mr. Budge, her history teacher, always kept his classroom extra warm with two heaters plugged in next to his desk.

"Ana — wake up!" whispered a friendly voice to her left. Ana opened her eyes to the smiling face of Nichelle Williams.

"Thanks, but I wasn't asleep," Ana whispered back.

Nichelle suppressed a laugh. "I know," she said, "but I could see you starting to nod off."

Ana put a hand to her mouth to cover a yawn. This was bad, she thought. Mr. Budge had been talking about what was going to be on Monday's test, and the blasting heaters had turned her mind into mush.

Ana forced herself to concentrate. Mr. Budge was busy drawing a map of the Louisiana Purchase on the blackboard. "In all the world, there is nothing so wonderful as a map," he said. "A map shows us not just where we are, but where we've been, and sometimes where we're going."

Although Ana found maps fascinating too, she was sure she could think of many far more wonderful things.

After class, Ana spoke with her friends in the hall. "Thanks for rescuing me, Nichelle."

"Another minute and you'd have been sawing logs like a lumbermill."

Ana laughed, then hit Blaine playfully on the arm. "Why didn't *you* tap me?"

"I didn't have the heart, you looked so peaceful. Besides, helping you catch up gives me an excuse to see you after school."

Ana blushed a little. "You don't need an *excuse* for that."

Blaine smiled. "So what do you say, Ana. Shall we head over to Eatz for a snack and a history lesson?"

"I can't. Nichelle and I are meeting Barbie and Chelsie at the *Generation Beat* office to talk about this skiing trip."

Blaine blinked. "I didn't know you skied."

Ana shrugged. "I don't," she said, "but Nichelle says she'll give me some pointers."

"Are you a good skier?" Blaine asked, turning to Nichelle.

"Well, I've only gone a few times, but I stay upright, mostly, and I've never broken anything. How about you?"

"I've been skiing since I was a little kid," Blaine said.

Ana looked surprised. "Brainy *and* athletic," she said. "Wow!"

Now it was Blaine's turn to blush. "It's the only sport I do," he said.

"Do you think you might like to come?" Ana asked, trying not to sound too hopeful.

"Are you kidding?" Blaine said. "Try and keep me away."

As Nichelle, Ana, and Blaine entered the *Generation Beat* newsroom, Tori was lecturing. "If you're not going to save your files in the computer," she said to everyone in the room, "you might as well go outside and write with your finger in the snow!"

"Did someone say snow?" Everyone looked up as Lara Morelli-Strauss entered the room. "I love the snow so much. Barbie, isn't it *fantastique*?"

Barbie came in behind Lara. "Hi, everybody," she said. "Looks like we're all here." She looked at Blaine a moment, then said, "Oh Blaine, did Ana tell you about the trip?"

Blaine nodded. "I definitely want to go."

"Anybody know who the chaperones are?" asked Nichelle.

"I think there are two or three teachers going along," Barbie said. "Ms. Krieger, the girls' gym teacher, is going, but I haven't heard about any of the others."

"You have now," called a voice from the doorway. The group glanced over as Mr. Toussaint strode into the room. In addition to his teaching functions, Mr. Toussaint also served as faculty adviser to the *Generation Beat* paper and website.

"Chaperone Number Two, at your service," Mr. Toussaint replied with a polite bow.

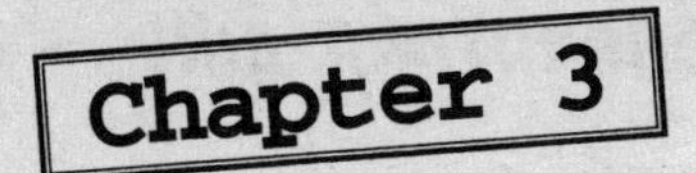

The Last Reindeer

At 181st Street Ana clutched her books and crammed into the crowded elevator that would take her from the subway trains to the street.

"Going up — watch the closing door!" shouted the elevator operator, a one-legged veteran named Roy, whom Ana knew from riding in his elevator almost every day.

"How's it goin' there, Ana?" Roy asked as the car bumped and whirred its way skyward. "You make the Olympic team yet?"

"Not yet," Ana laughed, "but I'm working on it."

The heavy door slid open and Roy yelled to the

waiting crowd, "Let 'em off, people. Ya can't get in until everyone's out."

Ana smiled as she squeezed past him. "Take care, Roy, I'll see you."

In the street, Ana gathered her wool coat around her. The snow had stopped, but an icy wind still blew. When she arrived at her building, Ana bounded up the stairs to her apartment door. A turn of the key later, she was standing in the vestibule inhaling the fragrant aroma of her mother's delicious cooking.

By the time Mr. Suarez came home from work two hours later, Ana, her mother, and Rosa had added the lights to the Christmas tree he had bought the day before.

"She's a real beauty," Mr. Suarez said admiringly. "Now all we need are the decorations."

Soon the impressive tree was covered with hundreds of tiny ornaments. As the final touches were being made, little Rosa disappeared under the tree's branches and emerged with a lovely ornament that had somehow been overlooked. It was a family favorite: a little hand-carved wooden reindeer with an elf on its back. Ana recalled that when she was younger the toy had been beautiful, with bright colors. Now the paint was gone in places, rubbed off from years of handling.

"Where did you get that ornament?" Ana asked her mother later as she helped her serve dinner.

"Which one?"

"The carved reindeer, the one Rosa loves so much."

"Oh — *that* one. Your father and I bought a whole set on a trip we took to Vermont for our tenth anniversary."

"Oh, yeah. I remember. I was real little and got to stay with Grandma."

"We had such a wonderful time," Ana's mom continued in a dreamy voice. "Your *popi* and I went for long walks in the snow. We built fires and snuggled together." Mrs. Suarez paused, blushing. "Well, anyway, one day a little old man came by our cabin with a cart full of Christmas ornaments he'd made himself. They were so beautiful we bought a dozen of them on the spot."

"A dozen? I only remember this one," Ana said.

"Over the years the others got lost or broken. This one is the last." Ana's mom sighed as she set a large plate of fried bananas on the table. "Okay," she said, turning to Ana, "now, please call everyone in to eat."

After dinner, Ana put Rosa to bed with a lovely Christmas story, then turned to her homework. She polished off her algebra problems in half an hour, then cracked open her history text. Just for fun she looked up a map of the United States and searched for Vermont. This was where her parents once vacationed, she thought. And this was where she hoped to go next weekend.

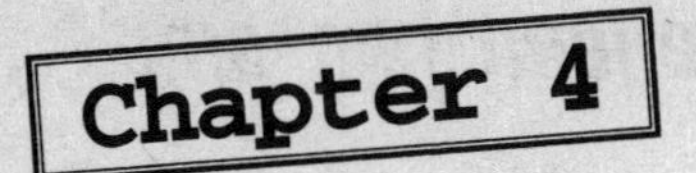

Leap and the Net Will Appear

After school on Friday, Ana found Tori seated at Chelsie's desk in the *Beat* office and watched as lightning-fingered Tori logged onto the Internet.

"Where's Chelsie?" she asked.

"She went home," Tori said, "Something about catching up on her sleep. I don't think she was feeling too sporty."

Ana looked concerned. "I hope she'll be all right for the trip."

"Crikey, me too," Tori said. "It's coming up soon."

Tori launched a search engine and found the site

for the ski resort, Powderpeaks. She clicked and then waited patiently for the resort's website to appear on the screen.

"Hey, look at this," she said. Ana pulled up a chair beside her.

"What *is* all that?" Ana asked, watching the swirling shapes and colors crisscrossed with jagged lines.

"Maps," Tori said. "Maps and more maps."

"In all the world," Ana said, imitating Mr. Budge, "there is nothing so wonderful as a map. What are these maps of? I don't recognize anything."

"They're maps of the Powderpeaks cross-country skiing trails, miles and miles of them. Say — look at this one!" Tori clicked away and the map grew larger, filling the screen with one jagged, winding trail. "That's an advanced trail."

"How do you know?" Ana asked.

"It's color-coded, see? Red's the most difficult."

"You know, a map *is* a wonderful thing," Ana said.

"And look at this — at the end of this trail is something called Dead Man's Drop. What do you suppose that is?"

"Search me," Ana said.

Tori double-clicked on the spot and a short blurb appeared in the corner of the screen. "Dead Man's Drop," Tori read, "used to be a favorite trail for advanced skiers, but was closed in the 1980s for safety reasons. Now it remains a scenic area with breathtaking views of mountain slopes and valleys."

"Sounds like a beautiful spot. Can we print out these maps?"

"Easy," Tori said, typing at the keyboard. In seconds a map came rolling out of the printer. It was an overview of the entire Powderpeaks area.

"Not much detail, Tor," Ana said. "Can we print out some enlargements?"

"Just leave it to me," Tori said.

While her friend clicked away, Ana took a yellow highlighter and traced a route from the Powderpeaks lodge to the top of Dead Man's Drop.

Presently, Barbie burst into the office. "Well — we're all set," she said. "It turns out that loads of people wanted to go skiing, but I pulled a few strings and got all of us in."

"That's great!" Ana said.

"Ditto!" exclaimed Tori.

"There's only one thing," Barbie continued, "we've got to get our money in by Monday, otherwise the ski club won't hold our places. Are you guys okay with that?"

"No problem," Tori said.

"Ana?"

"I think so," Ana said. "I'll make sure and call you tonight."

"Okay," Barbie said. "I'll talk to you then."

When Ana turned the corner onto her block that evening, she was surprised to see her mother and Rosa near the front stoop looking for something in the snow.

"Hi," Ana said. "Did you lose something?"

Rosa looked up and immediately burst into tears. "Oh, Ana, Ana," she cried, throwing her little arms around Ana's legs, "I didn't mean to do it."

Ana handed her books to her mother, bent down, and scooped up Rosa in her arms. "Hush, now," she said. "You didn't mean to do what?"

Rosa only buried her face in Ana's shoulder and sobbed. Ana appealed to her mother for enlightenment. "It's not the end of the world," her mom said with a shrug. "She lost her toy."

"Not the Christmas tree decoration?" Ana asked.

Her mother nodded silently as Rosa launched into a new round of sobs.

"She was watching Rudolph fly on TV," Mrs. Suarez explained, "and she wanted to see if her reindeer could fly, too. So, she dropped it out the window."

Ana stroked her sister's head. "Look, Rosita," she said, "I'm sure your toy will turn up when the snow melts. We'll keep checking every day. Okay?"

Rosa's tears slowly turned to sniffles. "Okay," she said bravely.

Then Ana got Rosa settled with a mug of cocoa and helped her mother with dinner. By the time she ate and helped with the cleanup, she felt completely exhausted. She went to her room, flopped onto her bed, and thought she might just have a good cry herself. While the meeting after school had gone well, she hadn't yet figured out how she was going to pay for the trip and still have enough money left to buy Christmas presents. No matter how many times she counted her savings, she still came up with the same number. It wasn't enough.

I'll just have to call Barbie and tell her I can't go, Ana thought miserably. She reached for the telephone, but before she could dial, there was a knock on her bedroom door. "Come in," Ana said, and her mother poked her head into the room.

"I'm sorry, darling," Mrs. Suarez said. "I know you're tired, but Rosa won't go to sleep. She's still upset about her toy. She says she wants to talk to you."

Ana hung up the phone and followed her mother into Rosa's room, where her little sister's face shone, streaked with tears.

"I was thinking about the little elf and the little reindeer lying in the snow," Rosa blubbered. "They must be freezing, and they're all alone!"

Ana sat on her sister's bed. "Well, you know something, that reindeer and elf have been friends for a long time. I bet they've had loads of adventures together, and this is just another one."

"What kind of adventures?" Rosa asked, no longer crying.

"Well," Ana said, "you lie down, get yourself nice and cozy, and I'll tell you one. . . ."

Twenty minutes later, Ana gently clicked the door shut on her sleeping sister's room. Her mother gave her a smile and a hug. "Thanks, *mija*," she said. "You are truly a star."

Ana smiled, but her heart grew heavy again as she dialed Barbie's number.

"Hey, Ana," came Barbie's voice down the line. "I was just about to call. Did you hear about Chelsie?"

"No," Ana said. "What about her?"

"She's got the flu. She can't come skiing."

"Oh no!" Ana said. "What bad timing."

"You said it. Her mom says she's got a fever of a hundred and three."

"Did you speak with her?" Ana asked.

"No, but I could hear her coughing in the background — it was awful."

Ana's heart sank. Nothing seemed to be going right. "Look, Barbie," she began heavily, "I've got some bad news of my own. I've been going over my finances and — "

"No way!" Barbie interrupted. "Pardon me, Ana, but I know what you're going to say and it's out of the question. You *must* come on this ski trip."

"But — "

"Look," Barbie interrupted again. "If you can't raise the money, I'll lend it to you myself, or Lara will, or Nichelle, or all of us put together. The point is — *you are coming with us on this trip.*"

"Believe me," Ana said, "I'm dying to go on the ski trip. It's just . . ."

"Ana, have you ever heard the expression, 'leap and the net will appear?' "

"Never."

"Well, it means if you really want to do something, you should just go ahead and do it, and let the details take care of themselves."

"Hmm," Ana said. "Leap and the net will appear, huh? I don't know, Barbie."

"See you Monday," Barbie said. "And don't worry."

The moment Ana hung up the phone, she heard a gentle rapping at her half-open door.

"Ana? Can I come in?" It was her father.

"Sure, *Popi*," Ana said.

"I hope you won't be mad," Mr. Suarez said, closing the door behind him, "but I was going past your room, and I — well, I couldn't help overhearing your conversation with Barbie."

Ana stared at him, speechless.

"Your friend is right, you know," her father continued. "Sometimes we have to take chances, do things that are in our hearts, even when they don't seem to make sense."

"You mean, like skiing?" Ana said.

"You're dying to go, aren't you?" Mr. Suarez asked.

Ana hung her head. "Yes, but not if it means having no money for Christmas."

Her father held up a hand. "I heard you say something about leaping and a net. Well, in this case, I am your safety net. The business is doing well. And if your heart is set on going, money is definitely not a problem."

"But, *Popi* —" Ana began.

"Not another word," Mr. Suarez said. "Merry Christmas, Ana," he whispered and blew her a kiss on his way out the door.

Ana sat for a moment on her bed, feeling close to tears. She often felt like crying when people were kind to her. But after a minute she perked up and reached for the phone again. "Barbie," she said when her friend came on the line, "I just wanted to tell you, I'm coming, after all."

Barbie laughed. "We couldn't do without you. Just remember to pack some munchies because it's a five-hour bus ride."

Ana pictured the little sliver of a state she'd seen on her map of North America. It was almost as if that little pink sliver was just waiting for her to come. She felt a sudden warmth and sleepiness come over her. She gave a big yawn.

"Hey, you still there?" Barbie asked.

"Yes, I'm here, but I've got to go. I'll see you Monday," Ana said, barely able to hang up the phone before falling fast asleep.

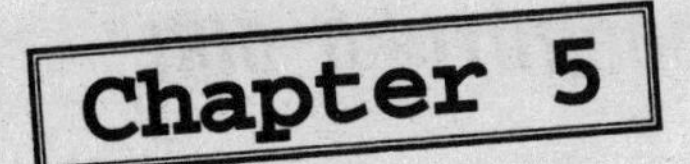

Learning to Stop

"May I have your attention, please?" It was Friday morning, the day of the trip, and Mr. Toussaint was standing in the front of a big chartered bus, straining to be heard above the roar of students. "Listen up, people," he shouted. "I have some announcements!" But even Mr. Toussaint's thunderous voice could not penetrate the din of sixty or more students chattering excitedly, rumpling bags of chips, zipping and unzipping, snapping and unsnapping backpacks, while trying to settle in for the trip.

Ana watched, amused, as Mr. Toussaint rolled

his eyes. He shook his head and muttered something to the bus driver. Evan and Andy — the Pants Boys — charged onto the bus, both looking as if they'd just fallen out of bed. Their hair appeared more unkempt than usual, while their shapeless pants seemed destined to drop right down to their ankles. They loped up the aisle, grinning at everyone, stopping to mumble at Barbie and Nichelle and with Randall Zaleski, whose hair shot out in clumps from beneath an undersized ski cap.

Ana also saw gangly Fletcher Minton talking with Melissa Larkin, the school's chess champ. Melissa and Fletcher were rarely seen apart these days.

Across the aisle from Ana sat a very happy Blaine, extra handsome and comfortable-looking in his ski outfit. She gave him a smile and he flashed one back, his perfect teeth gleaming at her.

"Looks like *everyone's* here," Tori said, rising in her seat beside Ana to crane her neck this way and that. "That's a dingo get up, mate!" she shouted to Lara, who stood in the aisle, wrestling a bag up into the overhead rack.

"Thank you, *cheríe*," Lara chimed, twirling once

gracefully in the aisle to model her jumpsuit. "I just bought this yesterday."

"I wish Chelsie were here," said Ana. "She's probably rolling around in bed with a fever."

"Poor thing," Lara said.

"Why don't we give her a call when we get to Powderpeaks?" Ana suggested.

"That's a bonzer idea," Tori said.

"May I have your attention?" Mr. Toussaint tried again, and finally everyone settled down enough so he could speak. He read aloud the checklist of kids who were going on the trip. "Did I miss anybody, except Chelsie?" he asked.

There was silence. "Okay, good," he said. "All present and accounted for." Everyone started to cheer, but Mr. Toussaint held up his hand. "Hang on," he said. "I have two quick announcements. First, Principal Simmons asked me to remind you all that we are traveling not only as ambassadors of International High, but also as representatives of our fair New York City. She asks that you all conduct yourselves accordingly.

"Ms. Simmons also asked me to remind you that Monday is a regular school day, just like any other.

There will be no special exemptions from homework just because you've gone skiing. We have a long bus ride ahead of us; I suggest you all make good use of that time. Any questions?" he asked. When no one responded, Mr. Toussaint smiled, turned to the driver, and shouted, "Okay, let's roll!"

An enormous cheer went up as the bus roared onto West Street, the beautiful Hudson River sparkling off to the left.

An hour later, after the singing had died down, Ana turned to Blaine. "How about giving us some ski pointers?"

"Gladly," Blaine said. "Now, the first thing you need to learn is how to stop."

"Shouldn't we learn how to *go* first?" Tori asked through a mouthful of pretzels.

Nichelle chuckled. "Trust me; *going* is never a problem on a ski slope. Soon as you drop off that chairlift, it's go, go, go — whether you want to or not."

Blaine frowned and said, "I don't think these girls will be going on any chair lift their first day, Nichelle."

Nichelle looked at him. "Why not?" she asked.

Ana piped in, "Yeah, why not?"

"Well, Ana, you're only a beginner. I think you and Tori better stick to the bunny slope for a while until you get the hang of things."

"Bunny slope? What's that?"

Tori made a face. "Sounds like something for little kids."

Blaine nodded. "It *is* for kids," he said, "and for beginners."

"These girls aren't exactly beginners when it comes to sports," Nichelle said.

"I know that," Blaine said. "But skiing can be dangerous. I'd hate to see anyone get hurt by being overeager. That's all."

Ana reached over and swatted him playfully on the arm. "Nobody's going to get hurt, Mr. Worrywart. Here, have a piece of fruit." She waved one under his nose until he smiled and took it.

"This is going to be a fantastic weekend," Tori said.

Ana sat back happily in her seat, looking out her window at forests of snow-covered pine. "It already is," she said.

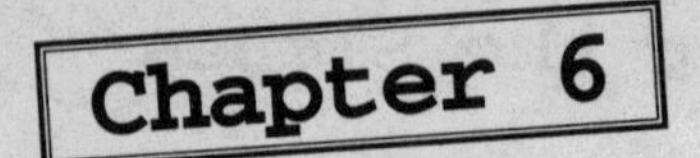

From Bunny Slope to Blue Square

When Ana stepped off of the bus at the Powderpeaks parking lot, she thought she might as well be on another planet. The late-morning sun sparkled off the mountains, which sloped to dizzying heights every way she looked. The crisp air in her lungs felt colder and cleaner than any she'd ever breathed. And sweeter, somehow, Ana thought, watching the clouds of her breath rise and break up like wisps of cotton candy.

"Well, what do you think, Ana?" A smiling Barbie appeared at her side, radiant in her green ski jacket and white knit cap.

"Oh, Barbie," Ana said, "it's incredible. I've never

seen any place more beautiful." She spread her arms and tilted her head back to take in the highest of the mountain peaks. "Barbie, thanks so much for insisting I come."

Barbie started to say something but gave a little shriek of laughter instead as a snowball thumped her shoulder, breaking in a spray of fine powder over her and Ana. "Hey!" she said, spinning to face the attacker.

A grinning Tori stood with her bag at her feet. "Are you two gonna stand there gabbin' all day? I thought we came here to *ski*!"

"So we did," Barbie said. "Are you ready, Ana?"

The bunny slope was pure chaos. Children of all shapes and sizes slipped and slid and tumbled this way and that. Kids were shouting, laughing — some even crying — while instructors darted after them, scooping up the fallen and trying to direct the flow of traffic up and down the broad hillside. Ana and Tori stood with Blaine and Nichelle at the base of the hill, taking in the scene with a mixture of excitement and trepidation.

"Do we have to start *here*?" Ana asked.

"Absolutely," Blaine said.

"But it's a madhouse," Ana said, watching a child Rosa's size crash into her father, both toppling head over heels down the slope.

"You should at least make a few runs here before moving on," Nichelle said.

Blaine shot Nichelle a disapproving glance, but she only gave him the same look back, imitating his expression so perfectly that Tori and Ana laughed out loud.

Blaine did not smile. "Now, pay attention," he said. "This is serious."

Ana giggled and this time it was her turn for a dirty look from Blaine. "Okay, Mr. ski-instructor," she said. "School us."

Blaine frowned, and Ana thought, *Why is he being so serious? We're supposed to be having fun.*

"Now, as I said," Blaine explained, "the first thing you need to know is how to stop. You have to 'snowplow.' Now remember, knees together, elbows tucked, tips of your skis nearly touching — Tori, are you getting this?"

Tori had gotten herself roughly in snowplow position, but just couldn't keep her eyes off the activity on the slope. "What?" she said, and then, "Oh, yeah. I've got it, mate. No worries." She twinkled a smile at Blaine but immediately focused again on the skiers zipping down the hill at every angle.

"What you want," Blaine continued, "is to lean forward and make a giant pizza slice of your skis in the snow, outer edges turned up, just like a pizza crust."

"I like that," Ana laughed, "ski tips for city girls!"

Half an hour later, Ana and Tori felt more than ready to give the bunny slope a try, but Blaine still thought more coaching was in order.

"That's perfect, Ana," he said. "You learn fast! Now, once you've got your form together," Blaine continued, "and once you've made it down the hill a few times in snowplow position, then we can talk about other techniques for gaining speed and control and — hey, where'd Tori go?"

Ana looked up, but saw no trace of her friend. "Maybe she went to the bathroom," she offered.

"Guess again," Nichelle said. "Unless I'm mistaken, that's our girl hitching a ride up the towrope."

Ana followed Nichelle's gaze up the bunny slope to where Tori clung to the fat rope, nearly slipping off as she tried to wave to them. In another moment she crested the hill, let go of the rope, and started downward, picking up speed with a little scream of laughter.

"She'll kill herself!" Blaine shouted, watching as Tori nearly fell over, then righted herself, arms and ski poles flailing every which way.

"If she does, she'll die laughing," Nichelle said.

"Snowplow! Snowplow!" Blaine shouted. Tori made a somewhat ragged pizza slice that nevertheless brought her skidding to a halt by her friends.

"That was bonzer! Primo! Magic!" Tori shouted. "Ana, you must try it! Ana?"

But Ana was already clinging to the towrope, halfway up the bunny slope.

"Ana! Wait!" Blaine shouted, catching sight of her. "You'll hurt yourself!"

But Ana only waved a pole at him, her skis nearly sliding out from under her as she did so.

Well, here goes nothing, Ana thought, as she let go of the rope and turned to face downhill. For a moment she felt light-headed, taking in the view, which, even from the bunny slope, was far more dramatic than what she'd seen in the parking lot. *But no time for sightseeing,* Ana thought, as she felt her skis sliding from under her. *Lean forward, lean forward*, she coached herself. *Pizza slice!* And the next moment, all the brightly-colored jackets and shouting people blurred together as Ana picked up speed and felt herself zooming downhill, so fast it took her breath away.

"Snowplow, Ana! Snowplow!" Ana heard Blaine shout through the whoosh of snow and wind at her ears, and she leaned forward, bent her knees, and pushed out her ankles, all of which slowed her down enough for Tori and Nichelle to grab her. The three girls twirled, spinning together for several yards before collapsing on top of each other.

"That was incredible!" Ana said, gasping as she untangled herself from her laughing friends.

"I knew it!" Nichelle said. "I knew you'd both take to skis like ducks to water."

"How'd I do, coach?" Ana asked Blaine, getting to her feet.

"Well, I guess you did okay," Blaine said grumpily. "You're lucky you didn't break your neck."

Ana gave him a hurt look. It was her first ski run ever and she felt thrilled to the marrow. Why was Blaine being such a pill?

"No one's breaking anybody's neck," Tori said

cheerfully. "C'mon, Ana. You ready for another go?"

"Definitely," Ana said.

Blaine frowned and looked at his boots. "Well, I guess I'm not needed around here," he said. "I'm heading over to the next slope."

Ana smiled, "Okay, Blaine, we'll see you over there," but Blaine didn't answer, skiing off toward a big sign with a blue square on it, which marked the intermediate slope.

"What's his problem?" Tori asked, as they headed for the towrope.

"I'm not sure," Ana said.

"Whatever it is, he'll get over it," Nichelle said. "Let's go!"

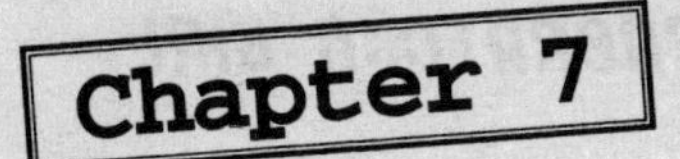

Life in the Fast Lane

Ana felt just the slightest twinge of apprehension as the three approached the chairlift that would carry them up the next hill, which was twice as steep as the bunny slope. "Now, *very important*," Nichelle said, "make sure you jump off the chair at the first drop-off, otherwise you'll be carried up to the black diamond slope."

"What's that?" Tori asked.

"That's the advanced slope." Nichelle could see the spark in Tori's eyes and said, "Don't even think about it, girl — at least not till you've tried the intermediate slope a few times."

Tori grinned ear-to-ear. "No worries, mate," she said.

Ana watched the chairs ride up the cable, no thicker than a telephone wire. They swung out into space, high above the snowy hillside.

"Get ready," Nichelle said, smacking Ana on the arm, "We're next!" just as a chair hit them in back of their knees.

"Hold tight!" Nichelle cried.

But there was no need to tell Ana, who had already gripped the steel bar between them with all her might. The chair rose sharply. It lurched and swung out as it cleared the first T-pole, and both girls gasped as they climbed higher every moment.

"Holy cow!" Ana said looking out over the bunny slope at the mountains. "This is incredible. How you doing, Tor?" she shouted.

Tori turned and waved. "Bonzer!"

"Look, Ana," Nichelle said, nudging her, "There goes Mr. Toussaint!"

Looking down between her dangling skis, Ana had no trouble spotting Mr. Toussaint's large frame streaking down the hillside below. "He looks good," Ana said, "like a pro."

"You see how he's tucked there, practically sitting on his skis?"

"Yeah?"

"That's what you want to do, especially if you feel like you're starting to lose control."

"I'll try and remember," Ana said.

"Now, if you really want to see expert skiing," Nichelle said as she pointed toward someone farther up the slope.

"Who's *that?*" Ana asked, watching someone in a bright yellow jacket come zipping down in stunning, graceful sweeps, banking left and right in elegant arcs.

"My goodness — it's Lara." Nichelle exclaimed. "Look at her go!"

"I bet she came right down from the advanced slope in one shot," Nichelle said. "Speaking of which, we'd better get ready; next stop is ours. Tori!" she shouted ahead, and Tori turned, grinning, to face them. "That's us!" Nichelle shouted, pointing with a ski pole. "Don't miss your stop!"

Ana watched the skiers ahead drop, two by two, from their chairs, tuck their bodies and bend downhill. But when it came to Tori's turn, Tori spun around, winked and waved at Ana, and remained seated.

"Tori!" Nichelle shouted, but it was too late; Tori had missed the drop-off and was already lurching skyward toward a sign with a big black diamond on it.

"What are we going to do?" Ana said. The drop was quickly approaching.

"I don't know about you, Ana, but I'm getting off. I'm no advanced skier. Get ready!"

But Ana shook her head. "Nichelle, I can't let Tori go alone. I'm staying on."

Nichelle barely had time to give Ana a wide-eyed "good luck!" before she jumped from the chair and tucked into position for her intermediate run.

"Ana!" someone shouted. She was just able to catch a glimpse of Blaine's shocked face, staring in disbelief at her, before she lurched up and away again, following Tori up the mountain.

"Now I've done it," Ana said to nobody, watching the advanced skiers shoot past below her. A familiar green jacket swooped by and Ana shouted, "Barbie!" She wasn't surprised that her friend couldn't hear her. That's the way, Ana thought, just like that. "You can do this, Ana," she said out loud. She watched more skiers, carefully noting their body positions and how they leaned into turns, transferring weight from one leg to the other. "You can do this," she said again, this time sounding convincing.

Ahead she saw Tori approach the drop-off. "Tori!" she cried and her friend spun around, surprised and delighted to see her.

"Ana!" she shouted, just before leaping from her chair, "I'll race yoooooooouuu!" Ana watched her friend spin onto the slope in a jumble of arms, legs, skis, and ski poles.

"What she lacks in form, she certainly makes up for in spirit," Ana said, feeling a rush of adrenaline as she neared the drop. "Okay — this is it! Steady now. Steady. One, two . . . THREEEEEE!" and she pushed herself off, landing flat on both skis, and immediately tucked into snowplow position for balance.

Wow, was all Ana could think, as she turned and took in the ring of mountains covered in snow, gleaming in the cloudless blue sky. For a moment, the sharp incline of the slope before her made Ana dizzy. But the next second, she shook her head, clenched her teeth, and crouched into position over her skis.

Almost at once, the speed she reached took her breath away. Ana concentrated, leaned as far forward as she could, locked her elbows, and shot like a bullet down the slope. The whoosh of snow and wind at her ears and the blur of trees and other skiers passing barely registered in her mind as she swooped down the mountain, concentrating with all her might.

In only a few hair-raising seconds, she reached the place where the ground leveled off for the intermediate run. She barely slowed down, hearing shouts and cheers she thought might be Barbie and Nichelle, before she zipped past them, bending low into the next slope. Just ahead, she spied Tori who, with no particular form or body position, somehow managed to stay upright. *Bet I can catch her*, Ana thought, and crouched back, squatting over her skis as she'd seen Mr. Toussaint do. Instantly she felt her speed increase and she cried out with glee as, in the next moment, she caught up with Tori, just as the ground began to level out again.

Tori gave a whoop of joy at seeing her friend in

one piece and, as the two slowed down, she turned and collided with Ana, both of them clutching each other, laughing uncontrollably as they came to a stop.

"We didn't even fall!" Tori said. "We must be getting the hang of this!"

A minute later, Barbie, Nichelle, and Blaine skied up.

"That was fantastic!" Barbie said.

"You girls were sensational!" Nichelle agreed.

But Blaine just gave her a sour look. "Ana, you nearly gave me a heart attack," he said. "I thought you were both done for."

Ana smiled. "To tell you the truth, so did I."

"Well," Barbie said, "if everyone's had enough excitement for the moment, how about stopping for a hot chocolate break?"

"That sounds good to me," Ana said. "Blaine?" but when she looked, Blaine had skied off by himself. She traded looks with Barbie and Nichelle, then said, "I'll catch up with you."

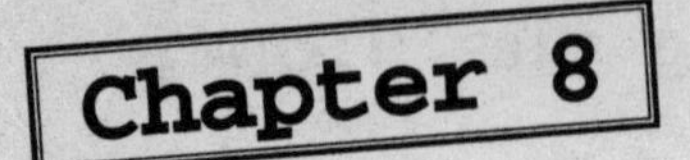

Wipeout

Ana skied over and found Blaine waiting in line for the chairlift. "Blaine, what's wrong? You don't seem to be having a very good time."

"You're right, Ana," he said, without looking at her, "I'm not."

"Well, do you want to tell me what the problem is?"

"The problem is that I'm just trying to teach you something, and you're so impatient. You won't even wait for one second."

"But I did! You taught me lots of stuff, and that

was great. And now I'm ready to have fun, so you can just relax a little, okay?"

"Okay, fine. You don't need any help from me. Fine."

"Look, Blaine," she said, "I don't know why you wanted to come on this trip, but I came here to try a new sport and to have fun. If you want to mope around and act like a wet blanket, you go right ahead — but you're not going to spoil my trip!" And she turned on her skis and pumped off after Barbie and her friends.

After a cup of piping hot chocolate with her friends, Ana felt better. The afternoon sun was already dipping behind the mountains, casting half the slopes in shadow. "Well, I'll see you two daredevils later," Barbie said. "I'm going to go try some snowmobiling."

"Well, what's next, Ana?" Tori said. "Want to make another run or two at the black diamond?"

"I don't know," Ana said. "I think once was enough. I saw a sign-up sheet for cross-country lessons at four o'clock. I think I'll go sign up, get the jump on things for tomorrow's hike." She looked at Tori. "You're still coming with me, aren't you?"

Tori shrugged and cleared her throat. "Gee, I don't know, mate. I was thinking about having a lash at the snowboarding. Any interest?"

Ana smiled at her friend. There was no getting around it; they were just plain different. "I don't know, Tor. All this zipping downhill — it's great fun — don't get me wrong. It's just," and she paused, thinking how she might explain, "it's just a little too much like the fifty-yard dash, you know? You get this huge adrenaline rush at the start, push your body to the absolute limit, but it's all over and done with in a few seconds, before you've even had a chance to enjoy it." She shrugged, spread her arms out to the side, "I can't help it — I'm a distance runner."

Tori smiled. "Fair enough," she said, and then, "Well, Ms. distance-runner, I'll catch up with you later," and the two friends hugged before going their separate ways.

"That's it, that's it," the instructor coached, "Right leg and left shoulder, left leg and right shoulder, plant your pole and pull, plant and pull — excellent!"

Now, this is more like it, Ana thought, already getting a feel for the rhythm and motion with the much narrower, much lighter skis on her feet. She and the other new skiers were circling a trail at the base of the mountains, just a little to one side of where the downhillers came zipping past to finish their runs. Ana saw Blaine come racing by, turn, and execute a perfect stop with a dramatic flourish of snow. She tried to catch his eye, feeling perhaps she'd been too hard on him, but Blaine pretended not to notice her and skied off in another direction. *Fine*, Ana thought, *go ahead and sulk if you want to.*

Nichelle skied over. "How's the cross-country going, Ana?" she asked.

"Pretty well. I think I'm getting the hang of it." She paused a moment, then asked, "I don't suppose you'd be interested in coming on a cross-country hike with me tomorrow, would you?"

Nichelle sighed. "I'm sorry, Ana. I feel like I'm just getting good at the downhill. I was even thinking of giving the black diamond slope a try tomorrow."

Ana smiled. "Oh, well," she said, " 'No worries,' as our friend would say. Have you seen her? She said she was going to try snowboarding."

Right then there were shouts and cheers from the slopes. Someone shouted "Go, Tori!" and Ana and Nichelle looked up to see Tori's blue jacket flying downhill on her board, arms spread wide like an eagle.

Nichelle shook her head. "Sometimes I can't decide if that girl's a complete maniac," she said, "or if she's really Superwoman in disguise — *uh-oh!*"

No sooner had she spoken than Tori slid off course, lost her balance, floundered one terrible moment, then fell. Ana and Nichelle watched, openmouthed, while their friend tumbled head over heels, bouncing, sliding, rolling down the hillside, with no sign of slowing down. Without a word, the two girls took off, racing to intercept her.

It seemed like every skier around came charging over to where Tori finally bounced and skidded to a halt in a heap at the bottom of the hill. Ana, on her light skis, reached her first. "Tori, speak to me — are you all right?" she asked, crouching over her friend.

A low groan escaped Tori's lips. Her eyes were closed, and for a moment Ana's heart sank with worry.

"Make way! Make way!" A uniformed medic with the Powderpeaks insignia on his jacket pushed his way through the crowd, and a second man hurried up, unrolling a canvas stretcher while the first man poked and probed at Tori. Ana backed up to give them room. "Nothing seems to be broken," the first man said to his colleague, and Ana breathed a huge sigh of relief. "Anyway, we'd better take her in and have her looked at."

The two men expertly slid the stretcher under Tori, lifted her, and skied off toward a cabin with a red cross on it. Ana and Nichelle followed, along with half the students from I. H.

Mr. Toussaint skied up, "Is she all right?" he asked Ana, a look of deep concern on his face.

"I don't really know. The medic didn't seem to think she broke anything."

"I'd better call her aunt," Mr. Toussaint said, hurrying to the first aid station.

That night, Ana sat alone at the desk in the room she shared with Tori, struggling with the intricacies of American government in her history book. She couldn't help glancing, now and then, at Tori's open pack, and at the clothes she'd flung hurriedly over her bed in her excitement to get out to the slopes.

There was an old-fashioned telephone on the desk, black, with a cord and a rotary dial. On impulse Ana picked it up and dialed Chelsie's number. "Mrs. Peterson? This is Ana Suarez," she said when she heard the proper English accent of Chelsie's mother. "Can Chelsie come to the phone?"

"Half a minute, dear," Mrs. Peterson said, "I'll just pop in and have a look."

Presently, a weak, stuffy-nosed voice came on the line. "Adda?"

"Chelsie? Is that you?"

"Yes, it's be," came the congested reply. "You're so sweet for calli'g."

"Are you feeling any better?"

"Ugh." Ana heard Chelsie blow her nose loudly. "A little bid," she said. "How's the ski trib goi'g?"

"Well, okay, I guess. Tori wiped out on a snowboard today."

"Oh, by," Chelsie said. "Is she okay?"

"I think so. They still had her flat on her back last I saw her, checking her out."

"I hobe she's okay."

"Tori's made of iron," said Ana. "Oh, listen — I'm sorry we messed up your desk in the *Beat* office."

"By desk?"

"Yeah, we were fooling around, downloading and printing out all these trail maps off your computer. I'm afraid with all the excitement we left things a mess."

"Adda, that's dorbal for by desk."

Ana laughed. "Well, I just wanted to check up on you, Chelsie. You get back to bed. Anything I can bring you from Vermont?"

"Yeah, bri'g a lead story for the holi'thay issue. I'b so drugged up with bedicid, by braid's dot worki'g."

"Forget that," Ana said. "Your only job is to get well in time for Christmas, okay?"

"Okay, Adda. Tha'gs for calli'g."

"See you," Ana said, and hung up.

Ana sat, staring into space for a minute. It was funny; she'd been so excited to come on this trip, so certain something special lay in this fantastic Christmas present. But now, between Tori's accident, Chelsie's flu, and her quarrel with Blaine, she just didn't feel even the slightest hint of holiday spirit.

I should have stayed home, she thought, but right then she heard the knob turn on her door and looked up to see a bruised but smiling face come in. "Tori!" she said, jumping up from her chair.

"Anybody need a cross-country skiing partner?" Tori asked. "I think I've had enough downhill for a while." And the two friends did a little (gentle) dance of their own, right there in the hotel room.

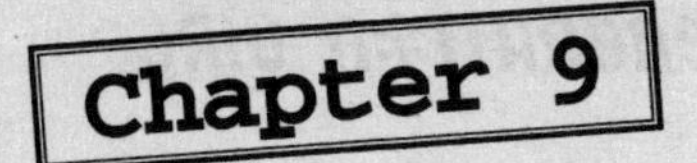

Missing!

10:20 A.M.

The sun was well up by the time Ana and Tori pushed off on the trail that would twist and climb gradually through the woods up into the mountains.

The trail they'd chosen rose steadily, dipping now and then into gentle downhill slopes where the girls could ease up and let gravity do their work for them.

"Crikey, I can see where this would keep you in shape," Tori said the first time they stopped to rest.

They'd come to a break in the trees atop a meadow that dipped and rolled to where Ana could just see the tiny rooftops of the Powderpeaks complex, far in the distance. "Wow, I didn't think we'd come so far already," she said, handing Tori an apple from her pack. She took out a trail map and traced their progress with a gloved finger. "We must be nearly halfway to Eagle's Point." The friends had talked and decided they still liked the shape of the trail leading to the head of Dead Man's Drop.

They munched their apples slowly, admiring the view they knew would only become more dramatic as they hiked onward.

"Look — a bunny," Tori said, as a rabbit the color of gray mist stopped to survey them. "Wonder if he'd like the rest of my apple?" she said and tossed her core to where the bunny sat sniffing the air.

Ana took a last bite and threw hers, too. "Well, if he doesn't, we'll have two apple trees here when we come back next year," she said. "Are you ready?"

"All set," Tori said, and the two took off again, with Ana leading, smoothing a trail for her friend who was still a little wobbly after yesterday's wipe-out. "Are we going too fast?" she'd turn around and ask every few minutes, but always Tori would smile and shake her head.

"No worries, Ana," she'd say, and they'd press on.

They'd started out in bright sunshine but as morning turned to afternoon, a bank of fat, blue clouds rolled in, blocking the sun, and the temperature dropped. Ana and Tori, both in down jackets, stayed toasty warm, especially with the rigorous pace they kept. But when they reached Eagle's Point, Ana felt a tickle under her nose and realized that the condensation of her breath had frozen on her upper lip.

"Say, what happened to our gorgeous day?" she said.

"Search me, mate."

"Oh well, it's beautiful up here," Ana said, looking over the acres and acres of snow-covered pine. "Still, I wish these clouds would blow over."

1:15 P.M.

Down below, Barbie turned to Lara in the chairlift beside her. "Brrr!" she said. "Is it my imagination or is it getting colder out here?"

Lara gave a little shiver herself. "No, you are right, my friend. I think it will snow today, yes?"

Barbie watched the clouds drifting in from the west and nodded her head. "Well, I guess the slopes could use some fresh snow," she said brightly. "But after this run, I'm going back to the room to grab an extra sweater."

"I go with you," Lara said. "Perhaps we grab, too, one hot chocolate?"

"Excellent idea," Barbie said. "We'll sit by the fire and warm our bones inside and out."

"But *atención*, Barbie. It is time to ski!" Lara said, and the two braced themselves for another drop down the black diamond slope.

2:10 P.M.

"Hey, is it snowing?" Tori said.

Ana looked up at the gray-blue clouds rolling across the sky. "If it isn't, it will be soon," she said.

The girls had stopped to rest at another lookout point, marked Sleeping Grizzly Shelf on their map. ("Hope that grizzly stays asleep," Ana had joked.) The view in three directions was stunning, except that most of the mountain peaks were now hidden in clouds.

"My little sister would flip if she saw this. Now I know why my parents spent their tenth anniversary in Vermont." Ana was quiet a minute, then she said, "You know, Tori, I was thinking, there aren't that many places for downhill skiing in Manhattan. But if we saved and bought some cross-country skis of our own, I know lots of places we could go for a good hike."

Tori smiled, "Really? Like where?"

Ana thought a moment. "Well, there's Central Park, and of course, Riverside Park. But to tell you the truth, when I think about it, I bet Fort Tryon Park would be best of all, and it's right near my house."

Tori said, "You know, I don't think I've ever been there."

"Really?" Ana said. "It's the highest point in all the city, did you know that? Chock full of beautiful, winding trails and scenic overlooks. It's great for sunsets over the Palisades — sunrises too, for that matter. I'll have to show you when we get back."

"Sounds bonzer," Tori said. "It's a date."

Ana sat with her back against a tree. "Well, it's snowing now," she said, and tilted her head to catch a flake on her tongue.

2:48 P.M.

"Wow, it's really coming down out there," Barbie said, staring out the lodge window, where even the nearby bunny slope was barely visible through the cascading snow.

"Yes. Perhaps we stay and have another chocolate," Lara said.

"Count me in," Nichelle said, who'd joined Barbie and Lara after taking a spill that had landed her right on her rump in the snow. "To tell you the truth, I think *this* skier's done for the day. Any more falls like that last one and I'll have to sleep standing up."

Blaine came in, his eyebrows and lashes thick with snow. He parked his skis in the rack by the door, stamped his feet, and strode to the girls' table by the fire. "Has anyone seen Ana?" he asked. "I know she went cross-country skiing with Tori, but I kind of thought she'd be back by now."

The girls all shook their heads.

"Maybe she's in her room," Barbie said. "Ana's the only person I know who might actually be doing homework."

"I don't think so," Blaine said. "I looked from outside and her light's not on."

"Maybe she is sleeping," Lara offered.

"With all that's going on around here?" Nichelle said. "That doesn't sound like Ana."

"Or Tori," Barbie added.

Blaine looked out the window. "I hope she's not still out in this," he said. "The wind's picking up out there; I think we're going to have a real snow-squall on our hands. This wasn't in the weather forecast."

"She's a big girl, Blaine," Nichelle said. "I'm sure she's all right."

Blaine sighed, hung his head, and slumped into a chair at the table. "Listen, Nichelle," he said. "I know I acted like a jerk yesterday. That's why I was looking for Ana. I wanted to apologize to her. But it's getting where you can hardly see your hand in front of your face out there. I'm really worried."

The girls exchanged looks. Barbie sipped the last of her chocolate and stood up. "Well, before we push the panic button, let me go check their room and see if we're not worrying ourselves for nothing. I'll be right back," she said.

3:05 P.M.

"Crikey, I've never seen it snow so hard in my life," Tori said.

"No worries," said Ana, who was quickly picking up Tori's expressions. "We have our shoe-snows on!" Tori looked at her blankly until Ana explained, "That's what Poogy calls snowshoes."

"Well, we have 'snowskis,' anyway, so I guess we're all right."

Nevertheless, the snow seemed to be falling thicker all the time. Ana stopped atop a small rise in the woods and said, "What do you think, Tor? Maybe we should start heading back. It's not like we're going to see anything from the lookout, anyway."

"Whatever you think, Ana." The accident of the day before had shaken Tori's confidence just enough that she didn't feel quite invincible anymore.

Ana pulled out the trail map, shielding it from the snow with her body.

"Well, remember, it'll be a lot faster going back, since it's mostly downhill."

"Right-o," Tori agreed, and the two turned in their tracks and started back the way they'd come.

Ana came to a rise, wind thrashing her cheeks, brought an arm up to protect her eyes, but simply could not make out the trail ahead. She turned her back to the wind, and Tori did the same. "It's no good, Tor — I can't see the trail."

"I know, mate — I can barely see *you* through all the white. What are we gonna do?"

Ana thought a moment, the wind howling at her ears. It was miles back to Powderpeaks. She turned and looked that way for just a moment, caught a blast of snow in her eyes and turned away again. "We can't go on this way," she said, raising her voice above the wind. "We have to find shelter somewhere."

"Any chance we could build an igloo?" Tori shouted, only half kidding.

"Not a bad idea," Ana said, "but I think we'd be frozen before we could finish it." Just a short distance back she remembered skiing through a place where the trees grew thickly together on either side of the trail. At the very least, she thought, those fat pines might provide some protection from the wind while they decided what to do. "Come on," she said, and the two girls pumped and pulled for all they were worth back up the trail.

3:51 P.M.

One look at Barbie's face told the others that Blaine had been right: Ana and Tori weren't in their room. "I asked about a dozen people on the way," Barbie said, "but nobody's seen them since this morning."

The lodge was filling up now as more and more skiers abandoned the slopes. Mr. Toussaint came in, parked his skis, stamped his boots and smacked the snow off his jacket and pants. "Whew," he said, striding cheerily to the fire. "So *this* is where you've all gone to. I was starting to feel like Jack London, out there all by myself." When no one responded, Mr. Toussaint said, "You know, Jack London? *Call of the Wild*? *White Fang*?" He surveyed the grim faces of Barbie and her friends and quickly asked, "What's wrong? You all look as if you've seen a ghost."

"Mr. Toussaint," Barbie said, "Ana and Tori are missing. No one has seen them since they left to go cross-country skiing this morning."

Mr. Toussaint turned serious immediately. "Anybody check their room?" he asked.

Barbie nodded, and Mr. Toussaint said, "All right, listen; everybody sit tight. I want you all to stay here till I come back."

"Where are you going?" Nichelle asked.

"To call the ski patrol, the police, the state

troopers — and anyone else I can think of to help find those girls."

He was halfway to the door when Blaine shouted, "Mr. Toussaint!" and the teacher spun around.

"What is it, Blaine?"

"Some of us are pretty good skiers," Blaine said, glancing at Lara and Barbie. "If there's going to be a search party, we'd like to help."

There were rapid nods of agreement from the girls.

Mr. Toussaint stared a moment at his students. He was proud of their courage and integrity. "Glad to know it," he said, and hurried from the room.

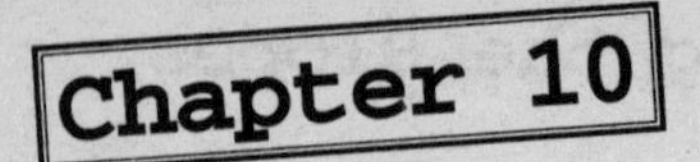

Chelsie Holds the Key

4:14 P.M.

"Get your skis off," Ana shouted, though her face felt almost too frozen to speak. "We'll be safe in here for a while." She pulled off her own skis and scrambled on hands and knees under the huge pine branches that sagged nearly to the ground with the weight of snow upon them. Tori crawled in after her. Instantly the two breathed a sigh of relief at being out of the wind.

In the ten minutes or so it had taken them to reach this copse of trees, the blizzard had worsened and the driving wind and snow had increased, until neither girl had any idea where the trail was. Ana thought it a stroke of luck to have stumbled upon this particular tree, whose heavy, snow-laden branches made a kind of tent. The ground was a soft cushion of pine needles and the girls sat huddled together, their backs to the tree trunk. For a minute they didn't speak but sat panting together, listening to the wind, letting their eyes adjust to the relative dark of their new surroundings.

"Crikey, Ana, that was quick thinking," Tori said when she caught her breath. "Another few minutes out there and we'd have been the latest frozen food, for sure."

"We're not out of the woods yet," Ana said.

"Maybe not," Tori said, "but at least we found our igloo — and we didn't even have to build it!"

Ana leaned her head back and stared up through the dark branches above her. It was no wonder that little Rosa liked climbing under the Christmas tree at home, she thought. Ana really felt safe here, protected by the sweet-smelling branches that circled her and Tori, like a mother's arms. Still, they couldn't stay here forever. While it was definitely warmer out of the wind, the temperature seemed to be dropping all the time, especially now that they weren't skiing but sitting still in the cold, huddling together for warmth. And the afternoon shadows were getting longer. Soon they would have to move on, Ana thought, or risk freezing to death. But where would they go?

4:20 P.M.

Barbie sat alone at the little desk in Ana and Tori's room. She'd wandered in, hoping she might discover some clue — anything at all — that could help in the search for her missing friends. She looked out the window, where gusts of snow still rattled the glass. If only there were something she could do. Her eye fell on the telephone, and she wondered briefly if she should call Ana's parents or Tori's aunt to tell them what had happened. No, the news would only upset them, and there'd be nothing they could do from New York, anyway.

She flipped through Ana's history book to a page covered with a map of Europe. If only somebody knew which trail her friends had taken. At least then they'd have some idea where to look. Barbie stared absently at the map a minute longer, then she had an idea and reached for the telephone.

Hitting the Slopes

4:22 P.M.

"Chelsie, are you awake, dear?" her mother called. "Barbie's on the phone."

"Yes, mum," she answered. "I've got it." She picked up the phone in her room, her head spinning slightly just with the effort of sitting up. "H-hello?"

"Gosh, I'm sorry, Chelsie, it sounds like you were asleep."

"That's okay, Barbie. I'm grateful; you rescued me from a rotten dream."

"Are you feeling any better?"

"I guess so. My mum's got me on these decongestants. I'm sleeping all the time, but at least I can breathe again. How's Vermont?"

"Oh, Chelsie," Barbie sighed. Chelsie could hear the worry in her friend's voice. "We're having a surprise blizzard up here. Ana and Tori went cross-country skiing and they haven't come back. Half the world's out looking for them; we're all worried sick."

"Barbie, can I do anything?" she asked. "Is there any way I can help?"

"Well, there's nothing you can do from there,"

Barbie said. "I was just wondering — and I know this is a long shot — but when you spoke to Ana last, did she happen to say anything about where she and Tori might be going on their hike?"

Chelsie's brain was cloudy. "Nothing comes to mind," she said. "She told me about Tori wiping out on her snowboard. Other than that . . ." but her thoughts were scattered. "I'm afraid I'm not being much help," she said.

"That's okay," Barbie said kindly. "It was a long shot, as I said. You go back to sleep. If you think of anything later, give me a call here at Powderpeaks."

"Will do," Chelsie said.

"And get well soon."

"Thanks, Barbie."

Chelsie lay back on her bed but she couldn't fall asleep. There was something nibbling at the back of her brain, something about her conversation with Ana yesterday. *What was it?* If only she could remember. . . .

4:24 P.M.

"Crikey, Ana, it's getting colder every minute," Tori said. Ana's eyes had adjusted enough to the dark that she could see the worry in her friend's face. "Don't worry, Tor," she said. "I got us into this mess and I'll find a way out." Ana opened her pack, pulled the trail map out, and spread it over their four knees. "Wish we had a light," she said, struggling to make out even the faintest detail on the map.

"Will this do?" Tori asked, pulling a key chain from her pocket and clicking on the tiny flashlight that hung from it.

"Tori, you're the greatest!"

"Present from Aunt Tessa," Tori said. "Never thought it would come in so handy."

Ana studied the map, moving the flashlight back and forth, up and down over the trails.

"Ana, I don't mean to sound like a boofhead, but what good's a map if we don't know where we are?"

"We may not know exactly, but I thought I saw something before on the map, right near the bottom of Dead Man's Drop — ah, here," she said, tapping the paper with the light for Tori to see.

"Look, a cabin," Tori said. "Do you suppose somebody actually lives there?"

"I don't know," Ana said. "Maybe it's just a decoration on the map. But if we find it, maybe we could get inside, whether anyone lives there or not."

Ana heard Tori swallow in the dark. "So, we'll be skiing Dead Man's Drop after all," she said.

"How bad could it be?" Ana said. "We survived the black diamond run, didn't we?"

"Barely," Tori said.

"Once we're down the drop," Ana continued, "it looks like just a short hike to the cabin along Beaver Pass."

"But how are we going to find Dead Man's Drop in the first place?" Tori said. "You can hardly see your hand in front of your face out there."

"Look," Ana said, pointing again at the map, "all these dark splotches indicate forest — see how there aren't any up on Moose Ridge?"

Tori nodded, "Yeah."

"The way I figure it, this big tree we're under must be here, in the dark splotch between Sleeping Grizzly Shelf and Eagle Point. All we have to do is head straight north, through the woods, and no matter where we are we'll intersect Elk Run — that leads straight to Dead Man's Drop."

"Sounds like a bit of a gamble," Tori said, and

Ana could see her grinning in the dim light. "Count me in."

4:32 P.M.

Chelsie tossed and turned, but it was no use; as tired as she was, she couldn't get back to sleep. What was it Ana had said to her? Something about messing up her desk. Something about her and Tori fooling around with trail maps — yes, that was it; Ana had definitely said something about downloading trail maps off the Internet. Chelsie sat up in bed, her blankets a tangled mess at her feet. If Ana and Tori had spent time looking at trail maps, wasn't it just possible they had left some clue as to what route they might have taken?

Chelsie kicked the covers off her feet. There was no time to lose. She stood up fast, grabbing the bedpost to steady herself as a wave of dizziness overcame her. "Yeesh," she said, "what a time to be ill." But then she thought, *it's because I'm ill that I'm here and not in Vermont. And that makes me the only person who might be able to help Ana and Tori.* Chelsie wobbled to her closet and began dressing as quickly as she could.

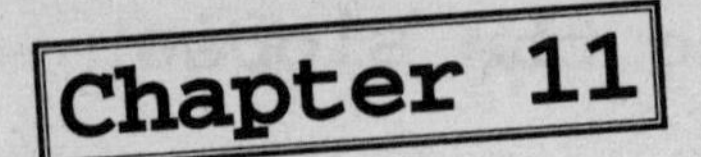

Dead Man's Drop

5:08 P.M.

The wind was howling and snow was still falling steadily when Ana and Tori came to a halt. Just steps from them, Dead Man's Drop plunged into a sheer valley of near-vertical slopes, the bottom of which was completely invisible through the swirling snow.

"Oh, Tori," Ana said, "I don't know. The black diamond slope was one thing — but *this* . . ." She let her words trail off in the wind. "We don't even have the right skis." She stared gloomily ahead. "You can't even see the bottom!" she said, hearing the fear in her own voice.

Tori looked her straight in the eyes. "Ana," she

said, "I know everybody thinks I'm a reckless person — and I admit, sometimes I am." She paused, tucking a wisp of hair under her hood. "But I really and truly believe we can do this."

Ana searched her friend's face but there was no sign of doubt. "Besides," Tori said, smiling ever so faintly against the wind, "what choice do we have?"

Ana looked out over the drop again, her heart and mind racing. Her feet and fingers were already going numb with cold. Fleeting thoughts and images charged through her brain. First teachers, for some reason: old Mr. Budge, with his ". . . there is nothing more wonderful than a map" — and how maps had helped her, at least so far. Mr. Toussaint's voice came to her: "At Christmas I no more desire a rose . . ." And wasn't it true? — *Snow* was the thing in season, the thing to be loved, and enjoyed, embraced, and endured, not in some abstract way, but right here, right now, even as it threatened her.

"Ana?" Tori tapped her friend.

But Ana's mind still raced along, with thoughts of her family now: little Rosa under the Christmas tree; her brother, Juan, so strong and proud; the beautiful, dreamy face of her mother as she described her wedding anniversary here in wintry Vermont; her father's soft voice wishing her "Merry Christmas." Ana thought of all the kind friends who helped her a hundred different ways: Lara, Nichelle, Chelsie, and Blaine, who, despite his faults, Ana realized, really was a good friend — oh, how she'd mistreated him! And at last her mind settled on Barbie, so kind on the phone that night, telling her — what was it? — leap and the net will appear. She stared out into the swirling whiteness and said aloud, "Leap and the net will appear."

"That's the spirit," Tori said. "Last one down's a rotten egg."

The two friends looked at each other a long moment. "Count of three?" Ana asked, and Tori nodded.

"Count of three," she answered, and together they counted, "One, two . . . *three*!"

The instant Ana pushed off down the slope, breathing became impossible. She held her breath, made slits of her eyes, and dropped and dropped through the swirling snow like a comet, picking up speed every moment. She bent low over her skis, bunched her every muscle into a tight ball, clenched her teeth, and shot like a bullet, the wind shrieking in her ears. A tiny bump in the slope launched her up so that for a second Ana was completely airborne. She gasped. Somewhere to her right she heard Tori shout, but Ana dared not lose her concentration as she landed solidly on her skis, regained her balance, and continued falling.

Another bump raised her even higher, and Ana feared she would faint with the sense of weightlessness for the second or so she remained aloft. Again she landed, slightly less solidly, but once more she found her center and somehow skied on, the whole world now a whistling, screaming hurricane of blurry white shooting past her. And still she held on, sliding, gliding down the mountain face.

Dimly, Ana heard a cry from Tori, who was slightly ahead of her, just a split second before hitting a bump that launched her this time far up and out into space. It seemed like forever that Ana hung in midair, not breathing, unable to see, jaw clamped shut, and eyes blurred. A strange, dreamy quiet was in her ears now as she flew through the air, completely disconnected from the earth. When at last she landed, she knew right away her balance was off. She felt herself slipping out of one ski, and when she tried to take weight off it, she instantly veered off course. Ana tried to compensate, veered back, and in one terrible moment, felt her legs go out from under her, as next she was sliding, sliding, full length on her side, down, down, down the mountainside.

5:15 P.M.

"Mr. Pugachev! Mr. Pugachev! *POOGY!*" Chelsie knocked and knocked at the glass of the janitor's basement window till she feared it would break. She knew that even though Poogy had an apartment of his own, he spent extra time at the school — just to make sure that everything was okay.

Finally she saw a light come on and Mr. Pugachev shuffled to the window. "What you want? Who is it? Go away!" he muttered.

"Mr. Pugachev, it's me, Chelsie Peterson. You have to let me in — it's an emergency."

Through the glass, Chelsie could hear the man mutter, "E-germancy, e-germancy. What kind e-germancy? Who is it? Go away!"

"Poogy, it's me, Chelsie — you know me. I

see you every day," she pleaded. "You *must* let me in."

There was more muttering, then she heard, "What Chelsie? *English* Chelsie?"

"Yes, yes," Chelsie cried, "English Chelsie. Chelsie *Peterson!* Poogy, I'm sorry to bother you but you must come and open the door for me. It's a matter of life and death!"

There was more muttering, then the janitor put his face right to the glass. "English Chelsie Peterson?" he asked. "Wait. . . ." Chelsie saw him grab his big ring of keys from its hook.

A minute later, the school's main door swung open, and Poogy waved her inside. "English Chelsie Peterson," the janitor said, "whatever is e-germancy, I help you," and the two of them hurried to Room 712.

5:18 P.M.

It might have been minutes, hours, or days that Ana lay in the snow before she lifted her head and realized, first, that she was alive, and second, that all her limbs seemed to be intact. She took off her skis and crawled over the snow to a dark shape that turned out to be Tori, lying in the snow. Ana stroked her head, brushed snow from her face, and her friend gave a low groan. "Tori," Ana said, gently. "We did it. We're alive."

Tori groaned again, opened her eyes, and smiled weakly at Ana. "This skiing's killing me, Ana. Can't we take up stamp collecting or something?"

Ana smiled back at her friend. "Can you stand?" she said. "We've still got just a little skiing to do."

Tori groaned but let Ana help her to her feet.

Ana could barely feel her toes anymore as she clipped back into her skis. "Come on, I'll lead," she said. "This Beaver Pass should lead straight to the cabin. Keep your fingers crossed," and she took off, keeping her head down, narrowing her eyes against the wind.

Right shoulder and left leg, left shoulder and right leg, plant and pull, plant and pull. If ever she needed to lose herself in a rhythm, Ana thought, now was the time. *Right and left. Plant and pull.* It seemed that her brain was going numb with cold. She glanced behind her and could just make out Tori's shape coming after her. She dared not slow down; their only hope was to keep moving and pray that the cabin was ahead somewhere. Before her all was swirling whiteness. *Left and right. Plant and pull.* The trail sloped upward, more and more, until Ana's legs began to tremble with the strain of climbing. Still she kept on and on; still Tori somehow kept up with her.

Just when she thought she could go absolutely no further, Ana felt the ground level off. A fierce blast of wind told her she'd come to the top of a rise, and she stopped and turned her back to the blast, waiting for Tori. There were so many things she wanted to say, but her jaw wasn't working. "Sorry," was all she managed when Tori brought her face to hers. "Sorry," she said again, through tears, "no cabin." But Tori only shook her head from side to side, raised an arm, and pointed with her ski pole.

Ana turned and, at first, saw only more of the thrashing white that blanked out everything else. But Tori jabbed excitedly with her pole and the next moment, Ana saw it, too: just ahead and to one side of the trail, something bright and yellow, shining ever so faintly through the raging storm. It was a lamp.

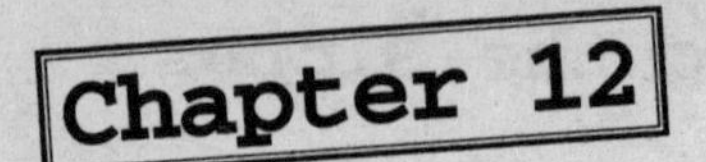

The Odd Couple

5:24 P.M.

"I knew it!" Chelsie said, "I just knew it!" Spread out on her desk were a half-dozen printouts, magnifications of Powderpeaks trail maps. She sifted through them and quickly found the one Ana had marked with her pen.

"Poogy, do you know what this means?" Chelsie asked, excitedly.

Poogy stared at the drawing over Chelsie's shoulder. "Your friend write on map. She go skiing."

Chelsie shook her head, impatiently. "Oh, Poogy — don't you see? Somebody highlighted this trail to Dead Man's Drop — I'll bet anything that's where Ana and Tori went on their hike! If we can just get word to the search party up there, they'll know exactly where to look."

Poogy raised his eyebrows, "Is good idea, English Chelsie. How I can help you?"

"Pass me the phone!" Chelsie said.

5:26 P.M.

"Oh, ho! What's this? What's this?"

Ana and Tori had pounded on the cabin's door for all they were worth for a minute or more before the door swung open and the girls tumbled in, collapsing, skis and all, in a heap on the cabin floor.

"What is it, dear?" asked a woman's voice.

And the old man, hovering wide-eyed and bushy-browed above them, said, "Eskimos, I think."

"Eskimos?" the woman asked. "What do you mean? Are they all right?"

But the old man was busy pushing the door closed, bolting it against the wind. "Poor things must be half frozen," he said, quickly pulling off the girls' skis and helping them, one at a time, to the hearth, where a roaring fire blazed. From where she lay on the hearth rug, Ana watched as an old woman appeared, white haired, like the old man, bundled in half a dozen sweaters of completely mismatched colors and at least three skirts of varying lengths.

The woman came closer, stooped, gently pulled the hoods of their jackets back, and unwrapped the ice-crusted scarves from their faces. "Good heavens — they're girls!" she exclaimed.

The old man scratched the scraggly beard on his chin. "Wonder why they're out in a storm like this?"

Ana's jaw was still too frozen to speak, and Tori was surely in the same condition.

"They must be lost," the woman said, then turned earnestly to Ana. "Are you lost?"

"It's no good," the old man said. "They must be tourists who don't speak English."

Ana wanted to reply. She opened her mouth, but suddenly the faces of the old folks, the rough hewn beams above her, and the dozen kerosene lamps flickering about the cabin all swam together with the blazing fire. Before she knew it, she was falling, falling into the deepest sleep she'd ever known.

5:48 P.M.

Barbie sat on the bed in her room and buried her head in her hands. If only there were something she could do. A gentle knock came at her door, and when she opened it, Nichelle, Blaine, and Lara all shuffled into the room.

"Come in, make yourselves comfortable," Barbie said. "I don't imagine any of us will be sleeping much tonight."

Everyone sat but Blaine, who paced back and forth from the window to the door, like a caged animal. It was now completely dark outside.

"Sit down, Blaine," Barbie said. "Being frantic isn't going to help Ana or Tori any."

"Barbie's right, you know," Lara said kindly, and Blaine slumped into a chair by the window.

"I just wish I'd gone with them," Blaine said. "If I hadn't been so pigheaded."

"If you'd gone with them, you'd be lost, too," Nichelle said glumly. "At least here we might still get a chance to help." She screwed up her face a moment, then said, "Does anyone else hear a phone ringing someplace?"

Barbie jumped up. "Goodness," she said, "it's my

cell phone in my bag — I forgot I even brought it." She reached for her bag and pulled the phone out, wondering who it could possibly be.

5:48 P.M.

When Ana awoke, the first thing she noticed was how quiet it was. It took her a minute to realize that the wind had stopped. The only sound was the crackling of the fire, still burning beside her where she and Tori lay, covered in several patchwork quilts of wild, clashing colors. She raised her head slightly from a feather pillow and looked about the large room. Beside her, Tori breathed softly, her eyes clamped shut in dreamless sleep. Heavy curtains covered the windows so that Ana had no idea what time it was. Her eyes moved to the little Christmas tree in one corner of the cabin, then rested on something she couldn't quite believe she was seeing. Could it be?

She rose from under the quilts, stood, and slowly shuffled, as if sleepwalking, to the tree. She reached a hand out to touch the object that had caught her attention. Sure enough it was a little wooden reindeer with a laughing elf on its back, almost exactly like the one Rosa had lost, except that this one looked freshly painted. Ana stared a minute in disbelief before she noticed the dozens of other ornaments adorning the tree's slender branches: elves and reindeer, swans and peacocks — even a little grizzly bear — all hand carved with the same delicacy and attention to detail.

The door opened from outside, and the old man came in, bringing a gust of cold air with him. In his arms was a pile of chopped wood, which he laid atop a stack by the fire. He nodded at Ana, smiled, then stuck his head through a door to another room and said, "One of them's awake, dear heart."

On the floor by the hearth, Tori stirred, lifted her head, and looked around, blinking in puzzlement. The old man watched her, then poked his head through the same door. "The other one, too," he added.

"Ask them if they're hungry," came the woman's voice, and the moment she heard the words, Ana realized she was famished.

"I'll try," the man said. "You," he said to Ana. "You, food, eat?" and he pointed a finger at his mouth, making lavish chewing and swallowing noises. His pantomime was so exaggerated that Ana laughed out loud.

"I don't know about you, mate," Tori said from the floor, "but I'm starved." She sat up, stretched a hand out to the old man, and said, "I'm Tori Burns — glad to meetcha. And thanks for saving us."

The old man's jaw dropped in amazement.

"I'm Ana Suarez," Ana said. "Did you make these?"

5:48 P.M.

"Oh, why won't Barbie pick up?" Chelsie asked desperately.

"Maybe is nobody home," Poogy said forlornly.

Finally, a familiar voice came on the line, and Chelsie shouted, "Barbie! Is that you?"

"Chelsie! What's going on? Shouldn't you be asleep?"

Chelsie quickly explained where she was and why. "And oh, Barbie — I think I know where Ana and Tori went skiing!"

"Tell me!" Barbie shouted.

"There's a map here that Ana marked with all the trails they were going to take! It could save the searchers hours of hunting!" said Chelsie.

Barbie gave a whoop of joy. "Chelsie, that's wonderful! Now, how are we going to get that marked-up map here? Wait, I know," Barbie said. "I have a laptop I can plug into any phone line. I've got my portable printer, too. If you fax me the map, I can print it out."

Chelsie felt instantly uneasy. "Mr. Pugachev," she said queasily, "do you know how to work a fax machine?"

But the janitor shook his head, "No, English Chelsie. I'm sorry."

Chelsie paled, felt her belly tying itself in a knot. "Oh, Barbie," she said weakly, "you know I'm no good with technical stuff. And this new fax machine seems so complicated."

"Well," Barbie said, "this would be a very good time to learn. The basic idea is easy: just put the map in the tray, pick up the phone, dial the number, and press 'Send.' I know you can do this. So first let me give you my number here. If I don't hear from you in ten minutes, I'll call you back, okay?"

Chelsie answered with a trembly, "Okay," and Barbie hung up. Chelsie stood up and wobbled over to the machine, the trail map clutched in her hand. "I don't even know which way the paper goes in," she said miserably.

Poogy shrugged. "So *try*, English Chelsie. If is wrong, you try different way, yes?"

Chelsie brightened a little. Poogy was right; there were only so many ways the map *could* go in the machine. "I've seen Tori do this before," she said. "I think it goes this way." She lay the map in place, dialed the number Barbie had given her, and waited breathlessly a moment. Nothing happened.

Instantly Chelsie felt feverish, a headache definitely on its way. "Now what?" she said.

Poogy looked a moment and then said, "I don't know. Look like machine is get no power."

It was true. Chelsie looked all over till she saw a little button that said POWER. "Of course," she said, "stupid, stupid, stupid," and she pressed the button, but still nothing happened. She felt like crying except that she knew that wouldn't do any good.

Suddenly Poogy laughed. "Oh, sorry, English Chelsie, I forget I unplug machine when I mop today. Try now."

He bent and plugged in the machine. Chelsie pressed the power button, and immediately the fax hummed to life. Poogy asked, "Is better now, yes?"

"Keep your fingers crossed," Chelsie said, and

dialed the number again. The machine beeped and clicked at her, then she heard the shriek of a fax tone, but again nothing seemed to be happening. She stared blankly; this time she really did feel like crying. Her head throbbed. A chill made her shudder and her eyes welled up with tears. *No,* she thought, *I won't cry. I can't let Ana and Tori down!* She glared at the machine before her. She felt like smashing it to pieces but instead, took a huge, deep breath, blinked back her tears, and concentrated with all her might. What was this little button here? She focused and read the word SEND. Send! That's what she had forgotten. She took another deep breath and pushed the button. . . .

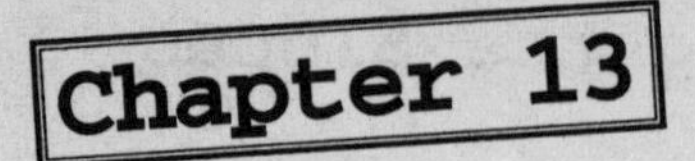

A Bad Turn of Luck

5:51 P.M.

"Lionel Romano's my name," the old man said, when he'd recovered himself. "My wife's name is Isabelle."

The old woman poked her head into the room. "How do you do?" she asked, politely.

"To answer your question," the old man said, "yes, I made all the ornaments you see. I'm a woodcarver by trade; used to make a good living at it. Nowadays, it's sleigh rides for tourists, sleigh rides for tourists."

"You have a sleigh?" Tori asked.

The old man laughed. "Well, how else would I give sleigh rides?"

"I don't suppose you have a telephone, Mr. Romano?" Ana asked.

"Oh, no," the old man said, as if the idea offended him.

"There's a ski resort just a few miles away," Mrs. Romano said brightly. "I'm sure they have a telephone you could use."

"Yes, that's exactly who we want to call," Ana said. "See, we were trying to get back to the resort when the blizzard blew in and we had to take shelter. If we hadn't come upon your cabin here, I hate to think what would have happened."

"Well, you're safe now," the old man said. "Soon as this storm blows over, I'll run you girls back to the ski lodge."

"Oh, would you?" Tori asked. "That'd be bonzer, Mr. Romano." The old man wrinkled his brow until Ana translated.

"What she means is, you're very kind," Ana said, "and we'd be most grateful for a ride in your sleigh."

6:08 P.M.

"That's it, Chelsie, transmission received — you did it. Chelsie?" For a moment, all Barbie could hear were the shouts and cheers down the line from the *Generation Beat* office. "Are you there?" Barbie asked, and eventually Chelsie came back on the line.

"Yes, I'm here, Barbie. Are you looking at the map?"

Barbie answered, "Yes. It looks as if Ana highlighted a trail called Elk Run, leading to a spot called Dead Man's Drop."

"I'm sure that's where Ana and Tori were headed on their hike," said Chelsie.

"I don't know," Barbie said, "after her wipeout on the snowboard, I'm not sure Tori would be up for something with the word 'dead' in it. Still, it's worth a try. Chelsie — you're a star. You may have just saved the day."

"Oh, Barbie, let's hope so. Is there anything else I can do?"

"Yes," Barbie said, "you can get yourself back home and into bed."

Chelsie laughed, still feeling light-headed. "Gladly," she said. "But promise me you'll call the instant you hear anything."

"I promise," Barbie said, and the girls hung up.

Now it's my turn, Barbie thought, when she got

off the phone. Her nerves were frazzled, but she knew that what she did now could make the difference between life and death for Ana and Tori. "Let's go find Mr. Toussaint," she said, "and see about getting hold of the search party."

6:39 P.M.

After Mrs. Romano had fed them stacks of banana-walnut pancakes, Ana and Tori bundled up, said a warm good-bye to the old woman, and followed her husband outdoors. The sky was still covered with angry-looking clouds. The snow had nearly stopped, but the wind was gusting furiously. Inside the shed, where the horse slept, was a long workbench covered with sawdust, small saws, and whittling tools.

"This must be where he makes the ornaments," Ana said, and Tori nodded.

"I'll run you straight down Beaver Pass," the old man said. "We'll be there in half an hour — tops."

"Hooray!" both girls shouted as they climbed up into the back of the sleigh.

The horse gave a sharp snort, Mr. Romano shouted, "Giddyap!" and the sleigh lurched forward with a sudden jingling of bells.

Tori turned, laughing, to Ana. "Looks like we get a taste of Christmas after all," she said.

"Talk about your one-horse, open sleigh!" Ana laughed back.

But soon their good mood began to change as the wind picked up and clouds started scudding across the moon.

"I hope he's right about the time," Ana said. "The wind's picking up again."

"Crikey, I'll bet the gang's worried sick about us," Tori said.

"Whoa, girl, whoa!" the old man cried suddenly and pulled the horse to a halt.

"What's wrong Mr. Romano?" asked Ana.

The old man squinted in the moonlight. "Looks like a big tree has fallen right in our path."

Ana and Tori looked at each other. "What can we do?" Ana asked.

"Well, we'll have to get around it some way." The old man climbed down from his perch, then stood rubbing his chin for a minute.

The two girls climbed down, and all three stood staring at the fallen tree, a mighty spruce that stretched fifty feet or more on either side of the trail. To the left, the ground rose in a steep incline to where the fallen tree's roots stuck up out of the snow. To the right, the ground dropped toward a treacherous ravine.

"Hmm," the old man said, rubbing away at his chin. "I suppose we might get around to the left if we all pitch in and help the horse with the sleigh."

"Oh, but Mr. Romano," Ana said, "even if we succeed, how will you ever get back to your cabin?"

"Ha!" the old man exclaimed. "I'll just have to get hold of a chainsaw down at your ski lodge and cut my way through."

Ana looked at Tori. "We'll bring our friends back and help you," Ana said.

"No worries, Mr. R.," Tori agreed.

"Hmph," the old man snorted. "I think we'd best cross that bridge when we come to it. Meanwhile, let's see what we can do to cross *this* one."

So, with the horse leading, the two girls and old Mr. Romano put their shoulders to the sleigh and began slowly pushing it up the hill to the left of the trail. At first, the operation went smoothly enough. Though everyone slipped and slid on the snowy hillside, their combined efforts were still enough to push the heavy sleigh up and up, till they'd nearly cleared the fallen tree.

Just when Ana felt sure they'd make it, a strange hissing sound made her look up, just in time to see a startled bobcat spring from behind a bush and go charging off into the woods. At the sight of the bobcat, the horse gave a loud whinny, reared up, lost its footing, and slid with a thump back against the sleigh. Ana and Tori were knocked clear, but poor Mr. Romano had no choice but to slide — sleigh and horse and all — back downhill, across the trail, and into the ravine below, where the whole circus crashed — with a great jangling of bells — into another tree.

Ana and Tori raced down the hill as fast as they could to where the sleigh had come to rest. It had completely flipped over and was wedged between two trees. "Mr. Romano!" they cried as they spotted the old man lying beside the sleigh.

"Mr. Romano, are you all right?" Ana asked.

"I'm fine," the old man assured her. "I just had the wind knocked out of me. How's the horse?"

As if in answer, the horse, who was still tied to the sleigh, gave an indignant bray and sat down heavily in the snow, raising one hoof in the air.

"I'm afraid he may have hurt one of his hooves," Tori called out.

Ana and Tori exchanged looks, then both glanced up at the dark sky.

"Now we're in a fix again," Tori said. "This seems to be the story today."

"You may just have to ski the rest of the way," Mr. Romano said, "I don't think I can make it."

"What — and leave you here alone?" Tori said. "No way!"

But Ana looked again at the sky and the dark clouds rolling past like angry giants above her. "Someone has to go for help," she said, "and quickly." She looked Tori in the eye. "I'll go," she said. "You stay here with Mr. Romano."

Tori started to protest but felt the wind picking up again and fell silent. Ana was right. If they stayed here, all three of them would freeze before long. Of the two of them, Ana was the better cross-country skier; it made more sense for her to go. "Okay, Ana," she said, "but you be extra careful, and take this," and Tori unclipped the little flashlight Aunt Tessa had given her.

"What's that for?" Ana said. "What am I going to see with that?"

"It's not to see," Tori said, "but to *be* seen," and she clipped the little light to the zipper of Ana's jacket. "Good luck," she said, and Ana hugged her before pulling her skis from the overturned sleigh, climbing back up to the trail, and taking off into the night.

6:48 P.M.

Barbie found Mr. Toussaint in the lodge, drinking coffee by the fire, and poring over a map.

"Mr. Toussaint," she began, "I have some information about where Ana and Tori might be." She spread the trail map on the table before the teacher and explained what Chelsie had told her. "Is there any way of contacting the search parties?" she asked.

"I believe so," Mr. Toussaint said and strode quickly to the main lobby, where police and state troopers were hanging around, walkie-talkies crackling at their sides.

After a quick discussion, one of the troopers got on his walkie-talkie and spoke in growly tones to the leaders of the rescue teams.

"Disappointing news," Mr. Toussaint told Barbie. "They've been focusing their search on the other side of the mountains. It will take at least an hour and a half to get to that other area."

Barbie was close to tears. "Oh, Mr. Toussaint," she pleaded, "can't we form our own search party?"

The teacher thought for a moment, then said, "Anyone know how to drive a snowmobile?"

"I do," Barbie said.

"So do I," said Lara.

"Me, too," said Blaine.

The Pants Boys mumbled and nodded in assent.

Mr. Toussaint nodded approvingly. "Okay, then, what are we waiting for? Let's move out."

The convoy of snowmobiles roared off in two directions. One pair of vehicles, led by Mr. Toussaint, with the Pants Boys following, took the high trail to Dead Man's Drop. The other pair, led by Barbie and Blaine, took the low trail. Both groups took plenty of blankets and each carried a flare gun so that whoever found the missing girls could let the others know the search had ended.

"Oh, Blaine," Barbie shouted above the noise of the snowmobile, "do you really think we'll find them?"

Blaine had been staring ahead, his jaw set, eyes scanning everywhere. The beam from their snowmobile cast ghostly shadows in the snow before them. "If they're out here, we'll find them," he said.

"But what if they're . . ." and Barbie swallowed hard, unable to complete her sentence.

Blaine looked at her. "Don't even think it," he said. He turned and knelt in his seat, shouting back to Lara and Nichelle, who were behind him. "Come on," he said, "everybody make some noise. And keep a sharp ear for anyone calling back!"

"AAAnna!" Barbie called. "TOR-reee!" And the others joined in, shouting their friends' names as loud as they could, the wind carrying their voices out into the night.

7:13 P.M.

Plant and pull, plant and pull. It seemed to Ana she'd lost all track of time and could say neither how far she'd come nor how far she had yet to go. The moment she'd left her friends, the night seemed to close in around her, dark branches creaking as the wind howled through the treetops. She thought of the bobcat they'd seen and wondered what other wild animals might be lurking about. The thought made her nervous, but she shook her head, bore down, and focused on the trail ahead.

"Left and right," she said aloud. "Plant and pull."

Breaks in the clouds overhead let the faintest starlight show Ana the way. More than once, she slid off course in the dark and narrowly missed tumbling into the ravine. "Steady now!" she coached herself. "Better to slow down a bit than risk falling." But each time she thought of the bob-cat, she couldn't help speeding up again.

Plant and pull. Left and right. When it seemed like she'd been skiing a long time, Ana suddenly skidded to a halt. It was difficult to see, but it looked like she'd come to a fork in the trail. She bent low to the ground, clicked on Tori's little flashlight, and, sure enough, saw that the trail split in two directions. *Terrific, now what?* she thought. Already her hands and feet were numb with cold. She felt for her pack, still strapped to her back, and pulled it around in front of her. If she could just get the map out, maybe she'd have a better idea which way to aim for Powderpeaks. She tried to open the pack, but it was no good; her frigid fingers couldn't undo the clasp. Ana watched her hands moving as if they belonged to someone else, but no matter how she tried, they just wouldn't do the job.

"Don't cry, don't cry," she said, feeling the tears well up in her eyes. "Tori and Mr. Romano are counting on me." She took a deep breath, chanted "Eenie, meenie, minie, *mo*," and took off down the trail to the right.

Her feet were gone. Ana couldn't tell where her hands left off and the ski poles began. She felt she was definitely losing her battle against tears as she skied on and on, the whole world now a wash of blurry white. *Plant and pull. Left and right.* But what was that? Faintly, above the howling wind, the creaking branches, and the rise and fall of her own breathing, Ana heard a sound, a low humming noise, soft but growing louder. And above the hum, was she imagining things, or was that a voice carried on the wind? But there it went again, and this time Ana knew she'd heard it, ever so faintly; voices — human voices, crying, "AAAn-na. TOR-reee." She did her best to blink back her tears and, in the next moment, saw the most beautiful thing she could ever have imagined: a string of brilliant lights, like a pearl necklace, or a length of Christmas bulbs, winding up the trail toward her.

The hum of snowmobiles grew louder.

"Here," Ana cried weakly and waved her little flashlight in the air. "Here," she cried again, and in another minute the snowmobiles came to a halt, directly in front of her. Four beautiful faces appeared before her, like angels in a dream, Ana thought. It took her a minute to realize it was Barbie, Blaine, Nichelle, and Lara, wrapping her in blankets, helping her off with her skis.

"Can you speak, Ana?" she heard Barbie say, but Ana could only smile through her tears as she heard a bang and watched a fireball of brilliant flame shoot, like a flaming star, up into the sky.

"Tori," she said, and pointed up the trail.

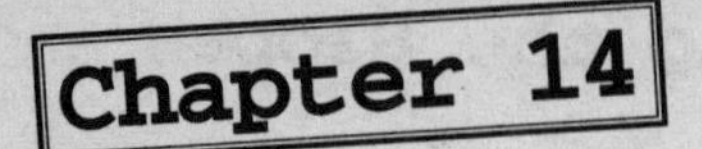

Blaine's Confession

After Ana and Tori called their families to tell them they were safe, they sat in their hotel beds, gulping spoonfuls of hot soup Barbie had brought them. The room was completely filled with I. H. kids, Mr. Toussaint, various uniformed police and state troopers, ski-patrol, as well as several Powderpeaks employees and skiers Ana had never seen before. It seemed like everyone wanted to have a look at the two girls who'd survived what one ranger called, "The sneakiest blizzard Powderpeaks has ever seen."

"All right, all right," Mr. Toussaint said eventually. "Let's clear out and give these girls some peace."

When most everyone had left, Blaine leaned in close to Ana. "Ana," he said, "I just wanted to let you know how sorry I am about how I acted yesterday, and how happy I am to see you're okay."

Ana rested her spoon a moment in its bowl, reached down, and gave his hand a squeeze. "I'm sorry, too, Blaine. I guess I overreacted."

"No, you didn't," he said. "It was me. I just thought it would be nice for once to be better at something than you — you know, to *help* you with something."

"But Blaine," she said, "that's ridiculous. You're good at so many things. You help me all the time. You don't have to be better than me at sports to be appreciated." Ana paused. "Anyway, I think I'm through with skiing, but would you still be my history coach?"

"Count on it," Blaine said, and flashed his brightest smile.

"Through with skiing? You and me, both," Nichelle said from her chair between the two beds. "I'm taking up ping-pong for my winter sport."

"Oh, I nearly forgot to tell you," Barbie said. "Chelsie called from New York. She's feeling much better and wanted me to thank you both."

"Thank us?" Ana asked. "What's she thanking us for?"

"For giving her the lead story she needed for the *Beat*'s holiday issue. She asked me to ask you both if you'd be willing to do interviews when you get back."

"No worries," Tori said.

"Fine with me," Ana said.

"I'll tell her," Barbie said.

Ana placed her empty soup bowl on the night-stand beside the bed. "What's this?" she asked, catching sight of a wooden box on the stand.

"Hey, I've got one, too," Tori said.

"Oh, those are from Mr. Romano," Barbie said. "When we took him home, he gave them to us to give to you. 'To remember our adventure,' he said."

"Like we could ever forget!" Tori said.

Ana opened her box and saw a set of beautifully carved, hand-painted ornaments, just like the ones she'd seen on the Romanos' Christmas tree. "Wow," Ana said, "these are gorgeous."

"And how," Tori added. "When I get home I'm sending him the best thank-you present I can find."

"Ditto for me," said Ana.

"Mr. Romano said to tell you his horse is okay,"

Barbie said. "Now, if you guys are feeling up to it, the bus home is leaving in about half an hour."

Ana still felt like she could sleep for a week, but the thought of going home to her own bed, with her family around her, gave her just the energy she needed to throw back the covers and stand up. "I'm ready," she said.

"Me, too," Tori said, and they both began packing.

Epilogue

The Number 1 train was packed, but Ana didn't mind. Everyone on the train seemed to be in good spirits, despite the record amount of snow still falling on the city streets. Christmas was just days away, and Ana had nearly finished the last of her shopping.

"Get yer poinsettias here! Get yer poinsettias!" yelled a gruff voice. Ana watched a burly man muscle his way through the crowds, a tray of poinsettia plants balanced over his head.

"How much?" Ana asked, when the man came near.

"For you, three dollars," the man said.

"Wow, can't beat that," Ana said, and dug in her pocket for the money. She didn't know whom she'd give the lovely plant to, but she felt sure she'd think of someone.

"Make room, make room," the man said, handing her a plant, then, "Get yer poinsettias — check it out," as he carried on through the train.

At 181st Street, Roy, the elevator man, was also in jolly spirits.

"Hey, Ana, you ever seen this much snow in your life?" he said, rocking slightly on his crutches.

"Only once," Ana said.

"Looks like there'll be no problem havin' a white Christmas *this* year."

Ana thought a moment, then took the bright poinsettia plant she carried and said, "Here, Roy, I wanted to give you something to cheer up your elevator."

The veteran took the plant with a big smile. "Gee, thanks Ana. I guess it does get a little gloomy in here sometimes."

When the doors opened, Ana started to exit, but Roy called her back. "Can we get going?" an irate passenger croaked.

"Hold your horses," Roy said, and waved Ana over. "It's not much," he said, "but I got a present for you, too."

He put something in her hand and Ana looked at it, amazed to see the little Christmas ornament Rosa had lost in the snow. "Found it on my way to work this morning, just sittin' in the snow on the sidewalk. It's kinda old, but somebody really done a good job makin' it, you can tell."

Ana thought of old Mr. Romano in his cabin up in the mountains of Vermont. She thought of all the people, friends and family, who'd combined to make this the most remarkable holiday season she'd ever had. She'd already wrapped up the box of ornaments to give as a present for her parents. Now she would be able to give little Rosa this treasure, worth more to her than anything Ana could buy.

"Can we get movin', already?" somebody whined.

Ana looked Roy in the face, bowed her head, and said, "Thank you, Roy. And if I don't see you, have a Merry Christmas."

"Merry Christmas, Ana," Roy said. "Watch the closing door!"

And as Ana stepped outside into the lightly falling snow, she thought how beautiful the snow truly was, and how, for all its trials and tribulations, this was already the best holiday season she'd ever had.

GENERATION GIRL™

available from Gold Key® paperbacks:

Book 1: NEW YORK, HERE WE COME
Book 2: BENDING THE RULES
Book 3: PUSHING THE LIMITS
Book 4: SINGING SENSATION
Book 5: PICTURE PERFECT?
Book 6: SECRETS OF THE PATH
Book 7: STAGE FRIGHT
Book 8: TAKING A STAND
Book 9: HITTING THE SLOPES

TURN THE PAGE TO CATCH
THE LATEST BUZZ FROM
THE *GENERATION BEAT* NEWSPAPER

SKI WEEKEND, A TEST OF NERVES

What would you do if you were trapped on a mountain in the middle of a blizzard? If you weren't a good skier, how would you find your way back to safety? Ana Suarez and Tori Burns know the answer because it happened to them!

On last week's ski trip along with sixty other I. H. students, these athletic girls lost their way on the ski slopes. To top it off, a monster snowstorm moved in, leaving the situation quite bad for Ana and Tori.

However, "no worries" prevailed, as Tori would say. They made it back alive. After incredible detective work by Chelsie Peterson, a daring snowmobile rescue led by Mr. Toussaint, and some heroics of their own, the girls were found safe. Now the whole group is back in Manhattan, right here at I. H. and ready for their next adventure.

IMPROVE YOUR WEBSITE

By now you've got your website up and running. Everyone in school is talking about how great it is. You've covered all the news that the kids in your school want to know about: sports events, parties, assemblies, everything! Now that everybody knows your website is out there, don't just keep doing the same old thing. The internet lets you add things to your website that are amazing, and you would never find this stuff in a regular, old-fashioned newspaper.

Add some of these features to your website to make it the hippest on the internet. Make your website even better:

- Add a calendar
  Create a calendar page listing important events at your school. If you want

to include a lot of dates, do a page for each month, with a link to each month at the bottom of each page. That way you can remind your classmates about tests, field trips, and dances.

- Illustrate stories with photos
  A photo on a website will catch people's eye and make them stop to read the story. Because photos are slower to download than text, be choosy when deciding which stories to illustrate, and always make the file size as small as possible.

- Add sounds
  It's not that difficult to add the sound of the crowd roaring to a story about your team's championship soccer game. All you need is a simple "helper application," a program that lets your computer do even more than it can now. Add the voice of the person you interview.

- Add a guest book
  Try including a guest book at the end of your website so that everyone who visits can add their name and leave a message. Ask people to tell you what they think of your newspaper. You'll get lots of new ideas that way.

Try these ideas with your school newspaper website and keep experimenting. Kids love reading about their school, their classmates, and what's new in their town. With these cool new additions to your website, you'll have more readers than ever!

HAVE FUN!

ALWAYS REMEMBER WHAT MR. TOUSSAINT SAYS:

WRITING=HONESTY=TRUTH

DON'T MISS **GENERATI*N GIRL** #10:

Chelsie takes a lot of pride in her work as assistant managing editor of International High's newspaper *Generation Beat*, and everybody knows she's great at her job. But when a co-worker steals her article she suddenly has a big decision to make.